Just Ahead Of Her In The Moonlit Darkness, A Figure Stepped Out Onto The Dock.

He walked to the far end, near the water. Then he abruptly turned and stared at her.

"Humans or black bears?" he called out in an amiable tone.

Jo drew up short at the sound of the voice at the dark end of the dock.

For a brief moment warm relief flooded her as she realized that Nick was all right.

But then she realized she'd just been set up. She'd bet all the gold in Fort Knox that Hazel was playing matchmaker, and if Nick Kramer was playing along, then he'd be sorry.

So very sorry, she thought as she stared at him in the moonlight.

"Skinny-dipping, my brave firefighter?" she asked.

His silhouette was clear, backlit by silver moonwash, slim-hipped and wide-shouldered. When he came toward her, moonlight illuminated his handsome profile, emphasizing th̶e̶ ̶ ̶ ̶ ̶ ̶ ̶ trician nose and hi̶ ̶ ̶ ̶ ̶ ̶ ̶ s.

Desire

D1462919

Dear Reader,

Revel in the month with a special day devoted to
L-O-V-E by enjoying six passionate, powerful and
provocative romances from Silhouette Desire.

Learn the secret of the Barone family's Valentine's Day
curse, in *Sleeping Beauty's Billionaire* (#1489) by
Caroline Cross, the second of twelve titles in the continuity
series DYNASTIES: THE BARONES—the saga of an elite
clan, caught in a web of danger, deceit…and desire.

In *Kiss Me, Cowboy!* (#1490) by Maureen Child, a delicious
baker feeds the desire of a marriage-wary rancher. And
passion flares when a detective and a socialite undertake a
cross–country quest, in *That Blackhawk Bride* (#1491), the
most recent installment of Barbara McCauley's popular
SECRETS! miniseries.

A no-nonsense vet captures the attention of a royal bent
on seduction, in *Charming the Prince* (#1492), the newest
"fiery tale" by Laura Wright. In Meagan McKinney's latest
MATCHED IN MONTANA title, *Plain Jane & the Hotshot*
(#1493), a shy music teacher and a daredevil fireman
make perfect harmony. And a California businessman finds
himself longing for his girl Friday every day of the week, in
At the Tycoon's Command (#1494) by Shawna Delacorte.

Celebrate Valentine's Day by reading all six of the steamy
new love stories from Silhouette Desire this month.

Enjoy!

Joan Marlow Golan

Joan Marlow Golan
Senior Editor, Silhouette Desire

Please address questions and book requests to:
Silhouette Reader Service
U.S.: 3010 Walden Ave., P.O. Box 1325, Buffalo, NY 14269
Canadian: P.O. Box 609, Fort Erie, Ont. L2A 5X3

Plain Jane
& the Hotshot
MEAGAN McKINNEY

Published by Silhouette Books
America's Publisher of Contemporary Romance

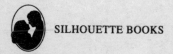

SILHOUETTE BOOKS

ISBN 0-373-76493-6

PLAIN JANE & THE HOTSHOT

Printed in U.S.A.

Books by Meagan McKinney

Silhouette Desire

One Small Secret #1222
*The Cowboy Meets His Match #1299
*The M.D. Courts His Nurse #1354
*Plain Jane & the Hotshot #1493

Silhouette Intimate Moments

*The Lawman Meets His Bride #1037

*Matched in Montana

MEAGAN McKINNEY

is the author of over a dozen novels of hardcover and paperback historical and contemporary women's fiction. In addition to romance, she likes to inject mystery and thriller elements into her work. Currently she lives in the Garden District of New Orleans with her two young sons, two very self-entitled cats and a crazy red mutt. Her favorite hobbies are traveling to the Arctic and, of course, reading!

One

"**Y**ou she-cubs need to think of something other than men and makeup." Hazel McCallum, the matriarch of Mystery, Montana, furrowed her brow in concentration as she continued speaking to the young woman sitting next to her in the car.

She slowed down for the empty logging truck that growled up the mountain slope ahead of them, then rambled on, "I know one goes with the other, but this trip's just for the gals. No men allowed."

"I wear hardly any makeup, Hazel, you know that. And as for men, I'm not exactly attracting them like flies to honey—with my bad luck, I'm not going to have to be reminded to put all my boyfriends in the toy box for a weekend." Joanna Lofton almost laughed. Hazel darn well knew she was the little gray mouse of Mystery, and that the matriarch was coyly trying to forget that fact made Jo's alarms go off.

"But all that girlie froufrou won't matter up on Bridger's Summit," Hazel rattled on, as if purposely not hearing Joanna. "There *might* be a few males up there, I suppose, but only if you count the bears, too."

"Bears?" Jo's eyes widened. The plain-Jane high-school music teacher was Montana-born and -bred, but even she was used to civilization. Her neighborhood in Mystery Valley was a world of cedar town houses and tiny tourist shops, with picturesque cattle ranches seen only from the road, Hazel's vast Lazy M spread included. Bears, rattlesnakes and other hazards of the wild were seldom encountered in the valley anymore.

The Bitterroot National Forest, in sharp contrast, was practically the old frontier untamed, and Jo was having second thoughts about letting her friend Hazel talk her into the trip.

Jo had agreed without really thinking about it. Hazel said the girls' weekend would do her good, perhaps get her out of the funk she was in. But there was never any talk of being mauled by wild animals.

"Did I hear the word *bears?*" Bonnie Lassiter interjected nervously from the back seat. "*Grizzly* bears?"

Hazel and Stella Mumford, the other woman who, like Hazel, was well into her seventies, laughed as if on cue.

"You believe these two youngsters, Hazel?" Stella teased. "You'd think both of 'em are from Manhattan. Bonnie, even a townie like me knows you'll find few grizzlies anymore in the lower forty-eight."

Jo glanced behind her to exchange a sympathetic glance with Bonnie. They were both the same age, twenty-five, and both from Mystery. Jo knew Bonnie was a divorced hairstylist who worked in Mystery Valley's most popular salon. They were also both starting to realize they had committed themselves to ten rugged days in the unfamiliar wilderness.

Hazel saw their covert glances, and a sly smile pulled at her lips.

The cattle baroness might have looked petite behind the wheel of her cinnamon-and-black Fleetwood, her suede driving gloves only enhancing the "little old lady" impression. But there was nothing fuddy-duddy about the seventy-five-year-old's driving skills, nor her fierce passion for Mystery, which was why she had embarked upon her latest endeavor of playing matchmaker in order to keep her beloved town young and alive.

"Move it or lose it, bull-whacker," she muttered, the Cadillac swooping out smoothly to pass the truck.

Jo tried to feel excited about the adventure in store for her. If she didn't know better, she'd have sworn Hazel was going to try to hone those matchmaking skills on her, but Hazel had described the Mountain Gals Rendezvous as a lot of fun and a sort of female confidence-building course. The older women, all "graduates" of the course themselves, no longer actively participated in the more-strenuous activities; they only supervised, letting the younger women take turns leading each other in a series of mental and physical challenges.

And no men were allowed. Hazel had made that clear before Jo would even consider coming. Jo didn't want a fix-up. After Ned, all she wanted was to lick her wounds and stay very far away from the flames that had burned her.

"Low country's in the rearview mirror now," Hazel said when the birch-covered foothills were abruptly replaced with steeper slopes and gradually thinning timber.

"Jo, I hope *you* at least were a Girl Scout," Bonnie declared, "because I sure wasn't. Only place I ever camped out was in the backyard."

Jo looked back at Bonnie, sending her friend a hesitant smile. "I think I know some heavy-duty survival skills—like how to roast marshmallows."

It was a harmless joke, but Jo's timidity seemed to irk the outspoken and hard-charging Stella.

"My goodness, Jo," she scolded mildly, "do you know you're so timid you even have a one-sided smile? Put your whole mouth into it! Pretty girl like you, it's a shame. *Where* did you inherit that shyness of yours? If I didn't know it for a fact, I'd never believe your momma was Miss Montana. Hon, when you've got a dazzling smile, don't hide it under a basket."

Jo realized Stella meant well. But the heat of resentment came into her face at yet another reminder that she lived in her mother's beauty-queen shadow, inadequate, a flawed colorless chip off the dazzling marble block.

Other girls were allowed to develop their own personalities, while Jo was expected to effortlessly replicate her mother's charming, gregarious, photogenic, always "on" vivacity. The ironic result was to make a naturally shy girl even shier.

"Never mind who was Miss Montana," Hazel interceded, sensing Jo's discomfort. "It's all history now. The point is, any gal needs a backbone, not a wishbone. The rendezvous is just what these town girls need to put some stiff in their spines."

Hazel's right, Jo tried to rally herself, the past is just history now. She was on a new road to a new outlook on life. The hurt couldn't count so much if there were no men around, even if that hurt caused by a cheating English professor in a midlife crisis left a hard, piercing sadness down deep where language couldn't soothe it.

At the sudden, unwelcome memory, Jo felt the warm and stinging threat of tears.

"Five more minutes and we're officially campers," Hazel announced as she swung the car off the blacktop road onto a narrow gravel access lane. Although bigger trees had thinned out, stunted jack pines closed in on the lane and cut off any distant view.

"Here, Jo," she added in an undertone, handing Jo

a faded but clean bandanna. "I think you got some dust in your eyes."

Hazel knew the main details about Ned. Neither woman believed there was dust in her eyes.

Jo managed a wistful smile. She still regretted her decision to come on this trip, but she knew she could at least fake enthusiasm for ten days out of respect for Hazel's good intentions.

The narrow access lane took them around the shoulder of Lookout Mountain to a remote campsite near Bridger's Summit, a few simple cabins without electricity, plumbing, or other amenities.

Jo could see a small clearing just ahead with only one car in it. But Hazel slowed the Fleetwood to a stop even before she reached the campsite, and no one had to ask her why.

Sun-drenched Crying Horse Canyon, visible as a deep gash beyond the cabins, lay below them, beautiful and serene. The Stony Rapids River cut a churning green ribbon through its middle.

But a few ridges' distance to the north of Bridger's Summit, dark smoke smudged the horizon.

Even as the new arrivals watched, a U.S. Forest Service helicopter hovered into view, dangling a giant bucket over a forested gulch below. The hinged bucket opened its steel jaws and bright-orange retardant misted into the gulch.

"Fire's still pretty far away," Stella remarked as Hazel pulled into the clearing and parked.

"Several ridges," Hazel agreed in a dismissive tone. "I've seen the fires come closer. Besides, before we left I checked the long-range fire conditions with the rangers. State weather service is predicting low winds and high humidity next few days, and those conditions don't favor the fire even if they say we might have to be evacuated."

Stella laughed, unloading the trunk after Hazel unlocked it. "They always have to say that, Hazel, my dear. It's a standard warning so you can't sue their butts for attractive nuisance."

"Attractive nuisance?" Jo repeated with a bemused smile, taking her knapsack.

"It's a legal term. You know, for something that attracts people to it, yet is dangerous. Like kids playing in abandoned refrigerators."

"Well," Hazel scoffed. "In my day, an attractive nuisance had big boobs and her eye on your husband."

She pointed with her chin toward the other car, a new beige Chrysler with Texas plates. "That Texas turncoat Dottie and her grandniece Kayla must be here."

Jo shook off her misgivings as she stretched her stiff muscles. The place was attractive, and as far as she could see, there were no nuisances at all.

Hazel gazed around the camp clearing for a glimpse of Dottie and Kayla, but still spotted no one.

"I rented those two biggest cabins right near the rim of the canyon," she explained. "One for age and

one for beauty. Looks like we have the place to our-
selves right now. Maybe the smoke scared off the
tourists.''

"Speaking of beauty," Stella muttered, gazing beyond the cabins to where a hiking path emerged into
the clearing. "Methinks I see Dottie's niece from Dallas. Talk about 'attractive nuisance.' Just look what
she's found in the woods.''

Jo, struggling under her heavy aluminum-framed
backpack, looked just in time to see a man and a
woman emerge from the surrounding pines and head
in their general direction.

The curvy blonde had to be Kayla. She wore too
much eyeliner for camping, and her denim cutoff
jumpsuit, hardly designed for practicality, revealed
long tanned legs and a glittering gold chain around
the left ankle.

Jo glanced at the man with her. His appearance was
a mystery. It was supposed to be a girls' weekend—
no men allowed. But the "talented" blonde had managed to find one in the woods, anyway.

"Hey-aaaay, y'all!" the girl called out in a cheerful
drawl, waving at them. "I'm Kayla. Aunt Dottie's off
down the slopes gathering firewood to cook supper.
Said she's starving.''

Kayla placed one hand on the man's left arm.
"And *this* handsome gent is Mr. Nick Kramer. We're
going to be invaded by men! Smoke jumpers, at
that."

Jo studied the tall, broad-shouldered, slim-hipped

man. Although athletic-looking in faded jeans and crewneck, he had a falcon-quick, alert gaze that evidenced a keen intelligence. He wore his cola-brown hair in a short brushcut; his eyes, she saw when he drew nearer, were amber-brown.

Not only was he incredibly handsome, she marveled, but he seemed most unaffected by it. Her experience with good-looking men—like Ned—had been that no woman could compete with their narcissism.

This man might not be vain, but that, she told herself, didn't mean he wasn't flawed in some other important area.

She covertly studied him.

One corner of his mouth pulled up a bit when he smiled, conveying self-confidence, cockiness.

Surely that in and of itself was a fatal flaw.

Finding her comfort zone once more, Jo dismissed her initial attraction to him as simply a brief surge in hormones following a dry spell. Besides, the last thing she needed on this trip was a man, handsome or not.

"Nick's not just a smoke jumper," Hazel interjected. "He's a Hotshot."

"Hazel," Bonnie objected in a murmur, "you're flirting with him already?"

Hazel and Stella both laughed, Hazel even slapping her thigh at Bonnie's ignorance.

"Hotshots," Hazel explained, still chuckling, "are the elite among the smoke jumpers, you goose. The gung-ho guys that get sent in closest to the source of the fire. Don't you watch the Discovery Channel? I knew it from that emblem on his shirt.''

''Glad to meetcha, Nick,'' she added, quickly making introductions all around. Jo felt Nick's gaze linger on her, and she fought the urge to squirm.

Jo knew she was no Kayla. Nothing fulsome and obvious about her looks, but she had never considered herself unattractive. She had inherited her mother's lucent green eyes and arching eyebrows, along with a shiny profusion of thick brunette hair that formed a widow's peak on a gentle, curving brow.

But that was where the mother-daughter comparison ended.

At five-two, Jo Lofton was petite like Hazel, in sharp contrast to Diane Lofton's leggy five-ten frame—legs just perfect for gliding with catlike grace down fashion runways in Paris and New York, as indeed Diane had until she'd married and settled down.

Long legs, Jo observed bleakly, much like Kayla's.

''Don't tell me we're in danger here, Nick?'' Hazel said.

''Not at the moment, Mrs. McCallum,'' he replied in a polite, pleasant voice. The musician in Jo immediately recognized a perfect baritone.

''Mainly we're in this area just to thin out a few green pockets,'' he added. ''There's cheatgrass down below in the gulches that provides good tinder for airborne sparks.''

Cynically Jo thought there was cheatgrass all

around in the world and not just the gulches, but she remained silent.

"We're not really going to be invading you," Nick continued. "I lead a twelve-man team that's in charge of monitoring Crying Horse Canyon, and we're using Bridger's Summit as our staging area. But we'll be downridge and we won't be in your way."

"Of course you won't be," Kayla said, flashing him a toothy smile wide as the Texas Panhandle. "What a neat coinkydink that we'd all end up here together."

Coinkydink? Jo thought, groaning inwardly. That's the way some of her sophomore female students talked.

Bonnie met Jo's gaze and rolled her eyes in an *oh, please* fashion.

"In fact," Kayla enthused, "why don't we all have supper together this evening? We could make it pot-luck!"

"That'd be great," Nick replied, his tone already squashing the idea, "but my team works twelve hours on, twelve hours off, and we go on duty in another hour. We work nights during the quarter of the full moon. It's cooler."

Kayla pouted, demurely touching her cheek with one of her elegantly polished nails. "The night shift sure ruins a guy's social life," she said, watching him from lazy, lidded eyes.

"We'll be seeing each other," Nick said, looking at Jo again with steady attention, which made her feel an inner tickle of nervous fear. "Right now you folks need time to settle in, so nice meeting you."

"See you later," Kayla called out behind Nick's retreating form. "How cute is *he?*" she said to the others in a lower tone. "Look at that trim caboose."

"He's a hunka-hunka burning love, all right," Hazel agreed, though her thoughtful gaze remained on Jo.

"*Never* get seduced by a firefighter," Stella warned sternly.

"Why not?" Kayla demanded.

"Because," Stella replied, deadpan, "every time you get hot, he'll beat you over the head with a shovel."

The corny joke caught everyone off guard.

They all laughed, even Kayla, whom Jo had to admit looked beautiful and confident when she laughed.

But moments later Jo's thoughts turned to Nick, the way his eyes had settled on her and refused to look away, the way his presence seemed to draw every female gaze like a vacuum. It had been a while since she'd wondered what it would be like to be held by a man, kissed and stroked. The very thought of it sent a neon sign of warning through her mind, but she still found herself wondering about the man Hazel called a Hotshot.

She knew one thing, however. The best way not to get burned was to stay away from fire.

And that, she planned to do the entire weekend.

Two

Kayla's great-aunt Dottie McGratten showed up only a few minutes after Nick left, both her arms filled with firewood and kindling. She had an old hickory-nut face, well seamed, under a startling profusion of snow-white hair, barely restrained by a Dallas Cowboys cap. The wife of a retired oil wildcatter and formerly from Mystery Valley, she was still as spry as Hazel and Stella.

"The old gals are going easy on us tonight," Bonnie observed as the three younger women settled into their cabin before supper.

"Yeah, but judging from their sly grins," Jo said, "it's only the calm before the storm."

"And it's going to be some storm," Bonnie said,

busy spreading her sleeping bag over the bare springs of her bed. "Star navigating, first-aid, fishing, rafting—if we survive this we'll get our Ranger Rick badge."

"You keep the badge," Kayla quipped demurely. "I'll take Ranger Rick."

Jo glanced around the cabin. There was an old iron stove with nickel trimmings, three metal bedsteads, one along each wall, and little else besides a few nails in the walls for hanging clothes.

Ten days, she thought. It didn't sound very long when she agreed to this. Now it loomed before her like a period of banishment, each day an eternity.

But she owed Hazel, if not herself, a cheerful attitude. McCallum money had financed McCallum Secondary School before there was even a Montana state legislature. And recently, since the hard-pressed state budget had virtually eliminated funding for art and music education, Hazel had almost single-handedly rescued the programs—and Jo's teaching position.

So what Hazel wanted, Hazel got, even if she had the addled notion to try to make an inept camper survive the wilderness.

"I have dibs on this," Kayla chimed in, flopping her blond self down on the thin mattress. She carefully arranged her cosmetics on a little wooden shelf beside the bed.

Bonnie turned to Jo and said under her breath, "She's got dibs on everything, inanimate or not."

Jo smiled distantly and placed her backpack on the middle bed.

Next to her, Kayla picked up a compact and examined herself. Her eyes rose to meet Jo's.

"Dottie says your momma was Miss Montana?" Kayla asked, her voice a little wistful.

There it was again, Jo thought, her mother's fame dredged up almost immediately by a virtual stranger. She felt a fist clench in her chest as she was reminded, yet again, that she dwelled in a perpetual maternal shadow.

"Dottie says right," Bonnie supplied when Jo refused to reply. "And she was one of the finalists for Miss America."

"Well…Montana," Kayla said dismissively. "I mean, that's nothing like being Miss Texas or Miss New York."

"Why not?" Bonnie demanded.

Kayla studied her face carefully in the compact mirror before she replied.

"Oh, you know. Big frog in a small pond. We've got so *many* pretty girls in Texas, so it's a real competition. But y'all in Montana got such an itty-bitty population." Kayla flashed a mouthful of stunning enamel at Jo. "Not that I'm saying your momma didn't deserve it. Shoot, I've seen pretty girls up north, occasionally, though winters up here will try a girl's complexion."

"We manage," Bonnie assured her, amusement in her tone.

Jo had realized that Kayla wasn't the brightest light on the porch. But as the dig just now proved, she was skillful at delivering stinging words in a syrupy tone.

Just like Jo's mother, who had believed she only had her looks to count on, Kayla was probably just as insecure. Even though Jo should have hated the curvaceous beauty, she just couldn't. There was too much about Kayla that was familiar.

"Officer on deck!" Hazel joked, stepping into their cabin. "Sorry to break up the gabfest, girls, but it's time for your work assignments."

"Work?" Kayla said. "I thought this was a vacation!"

Hazel cast a dubious glance at the redundant creams, lotions, toners, mask potions and other cosmetics crowding Kayla's shelf. "If we want halfway decent meals, it'll be a team effort," she replied. "Kayla, it's your job to gather firewood and kindling each day. Bonnie and Jo, you'll take turns hauling water.

"This is going to be an interesting ten days, ladies," Hazel predicted, adding, "One of you had better get water now. Dottie's starting supper."

Jo couldn't help wondering what Hazel was up to, for there was definitely some secret purpose behind her manner, her sly glances.

But the serene beauty of the Bitterroot country soon scattered her thoughts as she descended a looping path, the only sound the natural chorus of insects.

There were more trees as she descended, aspens not yet blooming gold, and narrow silver spruces. She reached the stone footbridge Hazel had mentioned; it arched over a narrow but deep-cut, bubbling stream.

It was peaceful on the bridge, beauty surrounding her on all sides, and she paused to enjoy the moment. Long, narrow shafts of sunlight poked through the overhead canopy of leaves, making silvery flashes of the minnows below in the creek.

A swarm of mosquitoes assailed her, and she suddenly remembered that her long hair, which because of the windy car ride she'd pulled into a ponytail and tucked into her blouse, was useless as protection.

Absently, Jo set the water container down and undid the two top buttons of her blouse. With graceful, languid movements, she reached behind her collar and pulled out her hair.

A masculine voice startled her. "Going skinny-dipping?"

She flinched, turning to confront the handsome smoke jumper who'd shown up with Kayla. Nick Kramer, that was his name. She remembered how his quick gaze seemed to take in every detail—the way a gyrfalcon studies a meadow looking for a little gray mouse.

She had to shade her eyes from the sun behind him. What with the sun blindness and the fact that his dark silhouette seemed to tower over her, she took an instinctive step back.

When his own gaze dropped south and lingered

there appreciatively, she glanced down and felt her cheeks heat with embarrassment. With two buttons undone, her blouse was wide open and gave him a good view of her bra and bare flesh.

"Can I help you?" she asked defensively, fingers fumbling to button her blouse.

"Me?" He almost seemed to laugh. "Usually I'm the one doing the helping."

"I asked if you needed some help. I did not say help yourself," she snapped.

"Evidently I should, judging from what I've just seen."

She felt the betraying flush all the way to her collarbone.

The corner of his mouth tugged. "Let me guess— you're a closet nudist? Hey, don't let me interfere with your free expression of—"

"I was not undressing," she flung at him.

"I'm sorry, then." His words were strangely quiet and wistful.

He was well over six feet and she had to look way up to meet his gaze. Being a townie and an academic, she usually only worried about intellectual might, but now, alone in the woods with a man who was strong enough and big enough to take without asking, she suddenly became acutely aware of her physical vulnerability. She took another wary step back from him.

He only flashed that self-assured grin of his. "I'm not following you, so forget the paranoia. I've got the same job you have."

He held up at least a half-dozen plastic canteens, all strung on a length of cord.

Seeing the canteens brought her back to reality. He wasn't some woman-hungry medieval maurader. It was the twenty-first century, and he would prove no threat at all if she just stayed uninvolved.

Reminded of her own task, she smiled her relief and picked up the water container next to her.

"After you," he said, holding out his hand.

She smiled again, the smile she used for students who irritated her, and headed toward a hand pump just past the bridge.

"Hey," he called from behind her. "Hazel introduced you as Jo. Is it just Jo—or something else?"

"Why does it matter?" she replied, her tone casual, her heart still beating as if she'd run a mile.

She didn't want to have a conversation with the man. After Ned, she was sworn off men, and her only reason for coming on this trip was to get away from the loneliness he'd left her with. Now here she was, in the wilderness, feeling like the only female on ladies' night at the Bullnose Barroom.

"It's Joanna, but you can call me anything you like, since I doubt we'll be seeing each other much," she answered breezily. "Believe me, you're here to put out fires, and I am definitely planning on avoiding fires."

She pushed down on the rusty hand pump. Putting all her weight into it, she still couldn't get it to move. It finally released with a bang, and she nearly fell over. Next she had trouble getting pressure built up in the thing; all she could get out of it was a series of gurgling, choking noises.

"Here, let me help you."

He gave the handle a few fast pumps, and clear water came gushing out.

"Let there be water," he quipped.

"Thanks," she muttered, nervous at the way he seemed to be crowding her. "I can manage it now."

But in fact it was difficult, once the container started to fill, to keep it up under the spout. It weighed a ton.

"Let me hold it for you," he offered.

Her instincts gone awry, she snatched the container from him when he tried to take it. Water splashed across her blouse, plastering the thin fabric to her skin.

"It's heavy, I just—"

"I—I can manage," she repeated, her mouth firming in a frown. "Don't you have a forest somewhere to save?"

She hadn't meant to be so cutting. But he exhibited all the signs of a fast mover, and no doubt with his good looks he had a woman in every national park.

But not her.

She had no desire to join that convenient, far-flung sisterhood of harem partners.

"All right, suit yourself." He stood back, still towering over her. "But you're sure wasting a helluva lot of good water."

She really was, too, for she was forced to let the container go lower and lower as it got too heavy, until most of the water was splashing onto the ground or onto her chest.

He just stood there waiting his turn, and she sent quick peeks his way, unsure if that odd contortion of his mouth was meant as a smile or a goad. The silence between them became painful, then excruciating.

She felt remorse for snapping at him.

"Well...thanks for your help," she said, giving him a light, uninvolved smile.

She'd meant to be polite, but her wooden gratitude rang a false note, and he seemed to detect it. She was halfway across the bridge, the heavy container bumping into her legs, when he said, "*Now* I see why you're the one fetching the water. It's so you can baptize everybody, right?"

She turned to send him a cold stare.

"Just a tip," he bit out. "When you decide to freeze out a man, make sure your shirt's not wet, because you sure don't look cold to me."

Her gaze shot to her chest. Her nipples were like hard buds, completely outlined in the sheer white fabric of her clinging shirt.

In shock, she lost her grip on the heavy water jug. It bounced and poured over her feet while she crossed her arms over her chest in a lame attempt to cover herself.

He laughed out loud.

Furious, she picked up the half-empty jug and

made to head for camp. She would just have to make two trips for water. And it would be worth it, because the next trip was definitely not going to include meeting him.

"Hey, come back," he taunted. "I like a challenge."

"Then stick to fighting fires because I'm not a challenge—I'm a zero possibility where you're c-concerned," she stammered, her teeth gnashing and chattering at the same time.

That goading twist of his mouth was back.

"Now that's a sure-nuff challenge!" he volleyed.

"No," she tossed right back, "it's advance notice to try elsewhere."

"I'm glad we had this friendly little chat," he shouted at her retreating back. "And you know what? I still feel the challenge in spite of your generous peep show!"

She almost spit she was so mad.

She hadn't spent five minutes with the man, and she couldn't remember being this undone.

So much for controlled and dignified academics.

Three

——

Jo noticed little of the waning day's beauty on her way back to the summit campground, for she was too preoccupied with angry resentment directed at Nick Kramer.

Big deal, so he was a smoke jumper—a ''Hotshot,'' at that. He figured women would be all over him, and perhaps they were.

Her brow furrowed. She didn't need this. She was still licking her wounds over Ned. It rankled her that she'd even noticed Nick Kramer—and his incredibly piercing eyes and his big athletic body.

His sexy voice, too.

She frowned.

She might as well admit it: she was angrier at herself than at him. At least she was self-aware. Being brutally honest with oneself in the company of the opposite sex was the only way to stay sane, and most of all, safe. And more than anything, she was determined to stay safe.

Her thoughts unwillingly jogged back to Nick. He wasn't vain but he sure was arrogant. Couldn't he have faked just a little humility? She felt her own mouth twist cynically. No, he'd probably scored so often he didn't need it. He struck her as the type who considered himself God's gift to women.

Just like back there at the pump—he acted as though he was doing her a favor by hitting on her.

The water container was heavy, and the return to camp uphill. She arrived back at the cabins out of breath, wet and out of sorts.

"*There's* our water girl," called Dottie, who had gotten a fire started in the outdoor oven and grill at the center of the clearing. "We were starting to think maybe you skedaddled with that smoke jumper."

Hazel, busy untangling a length of fishing line, glanced at Jo and immediately recognized the turmoil she was in.

"Here, let me wrangle that, hon," Hazel offered, and the seventy-five-year-old startled Jo by carrying the water container easily with one strong arm.

"We were just kidding," Hazel added for her ears only, "about you meeting up with Nick Kramer."

"Meeting up? Huh! I think the creep followed me to the pump."

"Creep?" Hazel repeated the word as if it was foreign to her. "Girl, either you need glasses or I do. If he was any better-looking, he'd be a traffic hazard. Here you go, chef."

She plunked the water down near the fire.

"Where's everybody else?" Jo asked, glancing quickly around.

As she spoke, Kayla emerged from the younger women's cabin, carrying a shiny little vinyl shower kit and a fluffy pink towel. She crossed to the big water container and began filling an empty plastic milk bottle, slopping water all over the ground.

"Go easy on that," Dottie snapped. "Jo didn't haul it up here so you could pour it on the ground."

"It's only water," Kayla pouted. "Jo, you don't mind if I take a little, do you?"

"Knock yourself out," Jo replied, totally uninterested in a clash with Kayla—the conflict with Nick Kramer had been enough for one day.

Dottie noticed Jo's frown and sent her a sympathetic smile as Kayla walked away. "I know you must be wondering why I brought Kayla. It's a crying shame, but she deliberately acts dumber than she is because she thinks men find it attractive."

"She's right—plenty do," Hazel cut in. "Hell, I love cowboys, but most of mine care only about boobs, not brains. They get nervous real quick when a gal mentions a book she's read."

"Well, anyhow," Dottie said, "Kayla doesn't mean to come off as irritating. At heart she's really a sweet and friendly girl. It's just that she's insecure. She works hard to keep all eyes on her. It didn't sit well to see that gaze go your way.''

''If you mean Nick Kramer's gaze, believe me, she can have him. I'm not playing the dating game anymore,'' Jo said.

''I certainly would be if I were your age,'' Hazel assured her. ''He's the bee's knees, all right.''

''He's horny, that's all,'' Jo stated bluntly.

''Horny as a funeral in New Orleans, most likely,'' Hazel agreed. ''So are you, but you won't admit it.''

Jo flushed.

''Besides,'' Hazel went on, ''that's not all. Give the man some credit. He does an incredibly dangerous job that has to be done. He's not stupid. He knows he can get laid. But I think he actually likes you, Jo.''

''What makes you possibly think that?'' Jo asked, incredulous.

''My gosh, hon, it would be obvious to a blind man. The guy's eyes lit up the moment he saw you.''

''And why not?'' Dottie demanded. ''A looker like you, he's just being honest.''

Right, thought Jo, honest—just like Ned Wilson, who praised her looks so much it embarrassed her. But what good was it to be called attractive by men who cared about nothing else but sexual gratification? Men who lied to get what they wanted, then returned to their families or took off for parts unknown? Her answer from now on was always going to be, ''No thanks.''

Jo mustered a mechanical smile.

Both older women were only being nice. But no matter how right she knew Hazel was, colorings of insecurity—even of inferiority—often tinged even Jo's brightest moods.

Plucky but pathetic—that's how she felt when she tried to act confident. Ever since Ned, trying to start over made her feel like a gunshot victim trying to whistle past a shooting range.

"Well, guess I'll finish unpacking," she said, mainly to end the awkward silence. Both older women watched her cross the clearing.

Dottie, who had known Hazel for seven decades, suddenly grinned.

"I've seen that look in your eye before, Hazel McCallum. What are you up to now?"

"Who, me?" Hazel feigned the innocence of a cherub. "I'm just happy for Jo, that's all."

"Happy! Crying out loud, she's all upset."

"She sure is," Hazel agreed. "And I *like* seeing her animated like this, even if it's negative emotion. That girl is too dreamy and unassertive. Sometimes she even comes off like a mouse. But Nick Kramer's got her all revved up."

Hazel's eyes narrowed. "I've learned to trust my instincts over the years where love is concerned. And right now they tell me that Jo is all wrong about Nick—sure, he's a hunk, all right. But the eyes are the windows to the soul, and I saw real depth of character in Nick's eyes. Despite what Jo may think, he's not the slam-bam-thank-you-ma'am type.''

Hazel said no more. Her mind was too full of machinations for conversation right now.

Nick Kramer and Jo Lofton struck Hazel as perfect for her master plan. She was on a secret mission that had become the passion of her twilight years: a mission to save her beloved hometown of Mystery, Montana, population four thousand and dwindling. Mystery, and the fertile valley it lay in, had been founded by Hazel's great-great-grandfather, Jake. But the longtime ranching community was changing rapidly as outside developers moved in, turning it into a summer-tourist mecca. More than anything else, Hazel feared that uncaring strangers would obliterate its original identity, making Mystery just one more indistinguishable hodgepodge of chain stores and trendy boutiques.

It would be a loss too great to be endured.

Sure, change was inevitable, but Hazel wanted it guided by love and vision, not profits.

So the matriarch of Mystery had come up with a plan: pairing natives who loved Mystery, as Jo did, with the kind of outsiders who would bring new life while respecting the old traditions—precisely the kind of unselfish man Hazel sensed Nick Kramer was. Greedy yuppies did not put their lives on the line to save forests and protect strangers. Hazel had a special affection for men who ''stood on the wall,'' as she described those with dangerous jobs.

While it was too early to know anything for certain where Nick and Jo were concerned, Hazel had developed a sixth sense around romance. She'd become a matchmaker, a second career that so far had produced three wonderful marriages. Her instincts had been instantly alerted the moment Nick and Jo had laid eyes on each other. As the playwrights phrased it, *the stage lit up.*

And where there's smoke, the matriarch punned to herself, usually you'll find some fire, too.

"Okay, you clowns, listen up," Nick called out as he returned with the canteens to his fire crew's base camp on Lookout Mountain. "So far it's been a piece of cake. Right now the crews on both sides of us are ahead of the fire curve. We've had enough humidity lately to make the flames lay down nice."

He tossed the string of canteens down.

"But the barometer is falling, instead of rising like it was predicted, and you know how those flames will roll over if the air gets too dry, especially if the wind kicks up. So tonight we take advantage of a full moon and thin out the green pockets down on the canyon floor."

"I got a better idea, Nick," called out his radio-man, Jason Baumgarter. "Let's go up on the summit and do a safety inspection of the cabins—a whole carload of babes is camped up there."

This suggestion was met with cheers and whistles.

Nick's twelve-man crew were seated around the hearty flames of a campfire, eating supper.

"Our fearless leader," quipped Nick's second-in-command, Tom Albers, "has already reconnoitered that situation topside, gentlemen. I saw him walking with a well-endowed blonde earlier, sacrificing himself for the rest of us."

"Yes, for my sins," Nick clowned, looking humble.

The fire crew jeered him good-naturedly in return, a familiar ritual. But despite the usual camp routine as the men prepared to go on duty, Nick felt a new distraction this evening, and she wasn't blond.

Rather, she was a dark-haired, green-eyed beauty with one hell of a chip on her shoulder.

Jo Lofton had intrigued him from the first moment he'd laid eyes on her. But unfortunately, the emotions she stirred within him dredged up other feelings, too, and memories he usually worked hard to quell.

Looking at women like Jo was downright madness for him, because it made him yearn for a lifestyle he wasn't sure he could live. Many people suffered from what was done to them, but Nick had discovered that his deepest scars were mainly scars of omission—the parents he never knew, the loving home he never had, the lack of any reason for putting down roots.

The one woman he had dared to let himself love, for whom he would have given up this nomadic job of his, did not let him make that choice. Karen had left him. According to her, she'd found something better. And her stubbornness triggered his own.

"Earth calling Nick Kramer," a voice said loudly, and Nick's thoughts suddenly scattered.

Tom Albers stood before him in the gathering light, buckling on his utility belt.

He stared down at Nick with a face taut with concern.

"You got a mind for this today? Last thing we need is a preoccupied man getting himself into trouble."

"I'm all right," Nick said, his jaw hardening.

Tom nodded. "How do you want us to insert?" he asked again. "Two teams or three?"

"Three," Nick replied, forcing dangerous thoughts of Jo Lofton out of his mind. "One north of the river, two south. It's too steep for vehicles, so we'll have to hike out. Each team leader radios me on the hour."

"Got it," Tom affirmed.

But as Nick rigged his ax to his backpack, Jo's taunting words snapped in his mind like burning twigs: *I'm not a challenge—I'm a zero possibility where you're concerned.*

Four

"Let's go, ladies. Rise and shine!"

Hazel's strong voice was like an explosion in the slumbering peace of the cabin.

Jo bolted upright in bed, wondering what the emergency was.

"Up and at 'em!" Dottie's twanging voice chimed in, loud enough to wake snakes. "We should be five miles down the road by now, cowgirls. Shake the lead out."

Still groggy, Jo groaned when a powerful flashlight beam swept into her eyes.

"My God, it's still dark outside!" Bonnie complained.

"C'mon, sweethearts, are you bolted to those beds?" Hazel said. "The wilderness is calling you."

"Okay, okay, we're up," Jo protested, although she couldn't help grinning when she saw the stupefied look on Kayla's sleep-puffy face.

Dressing in the dim illumination of an oil lantern, Jo donned the sturdy outdoor clothing she'd packed: blue jeans, red flannel shirt and sturdy high-top shoes. A splash of water to her face and she felt almost human. Brushing back her hair, she tied it into a ponytail and tucked it under her shirt.

While she tucked it, however, heat crept into her cheeks. She was recalling the scene yesterday with Nick Kramer.

I still feel the challenge in spite of your generous peep show.

In your dreams, bucko, she wished she'd retorted. Why did the good lines always come to her too late to use them?

As Hazel had promised, the day's new sun was just edging over the horizon by the time the girls, still knuckling sleep from puffy eyes, trooped up to the crackling flames of the breakfast fire.

Seeing the sun blaze to life, hearing the "dawn chorus" of hundreds of birds celebrating the arrival of daylight, Jo felt instantly buoyed. Her freshly renewed anger at Nick Kramer receded, and she felt a little thrill at the natural beauty around her.

She could see why this wilderness spot had grown on Hazel and her friends. "Back of beyond," Hazel called it.

"We're burning good daylight," said the wise matron gruffly when Kayla straggled in, inappropriately dressed in pink shorts and a midriff top. "We've got a three-mile hike down to the canyon floor and the river, so let's make tracks."

Jo hadn't realized how much her sedentary teaching job had affected her physical condition. After only thirty minutes on the trail—a series of looping switchbacks that descended to the floor of Crying Horse Canyon—she was short of breath. So were the rest of the younger women.

Yet amazingly, Hazel and the other two seniors were strutting out front, setting the brisk pace, joking and chatting and identifying various birds.

But no one was suffering the way poor, befuddled Kayla was.

Jo couldn't help feeling a little sorry for her. Her golden-braised midriff was already pocked with the swollen bites of pesky flies, and several times she had scraped her exposed legs on thornbushes. She even managed to snag her ankle bracelet while stepping over a downed tree branch. If Jo hadn't caught her in time, Kayla would have been sprawled facedown in the dirt.

"Break time," Stella called when they reached the halfway point, a little fern bracken with several fallen trees providing seats.

Hazel, in the meantime, seemed intent on studying the skyline to the north.

Thin wisps of smoke curled in the wind, and Jo

could hear the steady *thucka-thucka* of chopper blades as the Forest Service fought blazes in the adjacent canyons.

"Is the fire getting closer?" Jo asked Hazel.

"I can't tell," her friend admitted. "But it does feel like the wind's been rising, instead of dying down as predicted. And if you ask me, the humidity is down, not up."

"You can smell flames a little more, too," Stella said, taking off her floppy jungle hat to swat at flies. "And I'm guessing smoke has forced more insects into this canyon. I've never seen this many flies."

"I hope the fire *does* spread!" Kayla burst out resentfully. "I'm sick of this Danny Crockett stuff."

"Davy Crockett," Hazel corrected her, laughing in disbelief. "Some Texan you are," she added before leading the women to one of the quiet pools in the river.

"Bait your hooks," she ordered. "This is one of the best fishing holes west of the Great Divide."

"This is incredible!" Stella marveled after they'd been fishing for not even an hour. "The trout are practically leaping on the banks for us."

Even Kayla had gotten over her pouting. Now she seemed to be having the time of her life as she reeled in fish after fish.

It was especially remarkable, Jo told herself, because they were all "survival fishing," using just fishline and hooks tied to sticks—no fiberglass poles, no reels, only twigs for bobbers.

"Are they suicidal?" Hazel wondered as she tossed another fat trout onto the growing stack.

"It's the fires nearby, Hazel," a friendly masculine voice called out from behind them. "It's messed up the river ecosystem and forced a huge number of fish into other feeding habitats."

All six women turned to see an amazing sight: twelve men in their physical prime, all smudged and rumpled, all jockeying for a better view of the fisherwomen.

"Well, boys," Hazel greeted them with amiable irony, "am I *that* much of a sex goddess in blue jeans? Oh, I see—you've noticed the *children*."

"Mighty fine-looking kids, ma'am," one of the smoke jumpers cracked, and another added: "We do baby-sitting gigs between fires."

The men laughed, including Nick, but he also added in an undertone, "Manners, boys, manners."

His eyes found Jo's, and he sent her a friendly, let's-make-peace smile.

Despite being over her earlier anger, however, a mechanical smile was all she could muster. Especially with a dozen men ogling her—although Kayla, not surprisingly, seemed their primary focus.

"Y'all been puttin' out fires like big, brave heroes?" the blonde asked, waving at them.

"With our bare hands, sugar!" one of them assured her.

"We're off duty now," Nick explained. "We spent the night burning out some cheatgrass pockets—that's why we're smudged. No fires in Crying Horse Canyon. Now we're just hiking back to our camp.''

With twelve men and six women, neither Hazel nor Nick attempted any introductions. But no name tags were required—his men weren't bashful about breaking off into little groups to flirt with the women a bit before they left.

Jo wasn't in the mood for socializing.

She waded partway into the river and tried to look intently busy baiting her hook.

But Nick made a point of walking over to her.

"I'm glad I'm not that worm," he joked as she poked one with her hook. "I mean—you know, the symbolism and all."

She didn't like the way he seemed to crowd her. The river water was ice-cold and she dared not go farther out.

Her noncommittal glance only seemed to amuse him.

He tried another tact. "Look, I'm sorry if I came off a bit flip or smart-ass or whatever yesterday. That crack I made about you baptizing everybody—well, that was out of line."

"I see."

He shrugged one shoulder. When he replied, his tone wasn't quite so friendly. "No need to get all gushy with forgiveness."

Her cheeks heated. "Look, don't worry about it, Mr. Kramer—"

"I only came over to make conversation—"

"Actually," she challenged, leveling him a cool stare, "I don't think you're interested in conversation."

"I give as good as I get," he defended himself, his tone taking on a scalpel edge. "I s'pose you're a scrubbed angel?"

"More scrubbed than you," she returned, giving his soot-smudged face a once-over.

He stopped. Then as if suddenly finding the humor in her words, he tipped back his head and laughed. White, even teeth sparkled.

She found herself wanting to laugh, also, or at least smile. But instinct told her it would only lead her down the path to attraction, and then, destruction.

"Look, apology accepted, Mr. Kramer," she finished, dismissing him.

"You give every man that go-to-hell look?"

She glanced at him and must have given him another one, judging from the sneer on his face.

"Sorry I'm not some sober-suited, country-club accountant who never gets his hands dirty. I admit I haven't shaved in a while. I sleep in a tent and bathe in rivers, but it's hard work fighting a fire. And I didn't expect to meet some woman—"

She finally turned around and faced him.

His mouth formed a tight defensive line. His eyes were wary.

"Please don't think I don't appreciate your sacrifice," she said. "Many would be unable to fulfill even your smallest of tasks to fight a wildfire. However,

Mr. Kramer, this is a fishing hole, not a watering hole. If I wanted to meet a big strong man like you, I'd have gone to a bar, not gone camping.''

He stared at her, anger simmering in his face. "Know what? You need some serious couch time, lady.''

"Here we go again with your 'clever' double meanings. Your couch, I suppose?'' She lifted an eyebrow.

"I don't have one in my tent. But maybe you should see a shrink to deal with this man-hating thing of yours.''

A bubble of anger swelled within her. "Oh, I get it, sure. Any woman who fails to breathe heavy when the Hotshot comes around must not be a *real* woman, right? Well, I'll have you know that despite what you've been fed, a real woman's fantasy isn't to be picked up and carried off into the sunset. We've figured out men like you. You'll be right back here trying to pick up another woman to carry off tomorrow night. So thanks, but no thanks.''

Fury sparked in his amber-brown eyes.

But before he could retort, the two of them realized something simultaneously: how silent the area had suddenly become.

Heat again leaped into her face and neck when she glanced at the others.

In the peak of anger she and Nick had spoken too loudly—all the rest were avidly listening, waiting for more.

A teasing cheer broke out.

"Damn you, are you happy?" she whispered at him.

"Smooth technique, Romeo," one of the smoke jumpers called over. "She's eating from your hand, stud! We're all taking notes here, chief."

"Way to go, Nick!" another one regaled him. "You've snatched defeat from the jaws of victory!"

Nick, clearly still angry, turned and walked away.

Jo tried to return to fishing. But when her pole suddenly jerked with a hooked fish, she was caught off balance. She fell into the knee-deep icy water, her line almost towing her across the pool.

Her cry of surprise and dismay triggered more laughter.

But Nick wasn't laughing. Instead, he was at her side, pulling her to her feet.

Wet from the collar down, bone-cold from the glacial stream, she could barely utter a thanks between her chattering teeth.

He met her gaze, his arm like a post, steadying her.

"Men like me have their place in this world. You'd do well to remember it," he said for her ears only.

"I don't need a rescuer," she insisted breathlessly.

He dropped his hold on her, and she wished he hadn't. On her own in the shallow rock-bottom pool, she realized how unsteady she was.

"This'd be yours, I think," he said, holding out the huge trout on her fishing line.

Wet, speechless, chagrined, she took the trout.

His gaze flicked downward to her water-plastered red flannel shirt.

She didn't need to look herself. She could feel how cold and hard her nipples were. At the rate she was revealing herself to him, she'd be naked by their next meeting.

"Yeah, maybe you're right," he said, his tone pensive and bitter. "Maybe I'm the one who needs rescuing." He sounded as if he was admitting to some kind of deep, forlorn ache.

He left her standing alone in the pool. But as he ordered his men to hit the trail again, a slyly smiling Hazel piped up.

"Say, boys! Since the fires have sent us this bounty of fish, why don't you stop by our camp this evening for a fish bake before you go on duty?"

"We've got far more than we can eat," Kayla added. "Shame to waste it, guys."

"That's certainly gracious of you ladies," Nick agreed. "Gives us a break from freeze-dried food. Thank you. We'll be there."

He and Jo pointedly avoided looking at each other—a fact that made Hazel's smile stretch even wider.

She hadn't come up here expecting to make another match. But then again, thought the matriarch, the essence of "luck" was merely the readiness to seize a good opportunity.

Nick Kramer and Joanna Lofton were getting along like a cobra and a mongoose. So far.

But nothing made Hazel more hopeful than seeing a young couple with deep wells of inner feeling—she had heard it just now, unmistakably, in both their voices.

Either it would all blow up in Hazel's face, or she would secure one more marriage and another fine family for Mystery's dwindling population.

No middle ground here, she predicted, watching Jo gather up her catch, still frowning.

They'd either become passionate lovers or mortal enemies.

Just which outcome, however, was still too hard to call.

Five

"There's nothing to it," Dottie McGratten called out. "You lop off the head, lop off the tail, then just split and scoop. Shouldn't take you more than thirty seconds."

Jo, Bonnie and Kayla were all cleaning fish on tree stumps, getting a quick lesson from Dottie. Kayla covered her eyes as Dottie scooped out the insides of her demonstration trout.

"That is so gross!" Kayla protested. "What's next, we watch sausage being made?"

Hazel, busy building a fire in the outside grill, laughed at Kayla's squeamishness.

"Good lands, city slicker! You think fish filet themselves? If you think this is gross, what if you were starving and had to butcher a cow?"

"I'd buy a frozen entrée," Kayla flung back, for by now she had evidently decided that Hazel was picking on her.

"Better get to it," Stella urged Kayla. "You want our guests to go hungry? Won't be long, there'll be a dozen hungry firefighters descending on this place."

"Yes," Bonnie chimed in, "I'll bet their 'appetites' are strong, all right."

"All you youngsters be careful around those guys," Hazel warned. "They're fine young men, I don't doubt, but they all suffer from the Hawaiian Disease."

Jo frowned. "What's Hawaiian Disease?"

"Lackanooky," Hazel replied, deadpan.

Young and old, Kayla included, all six women burst out laughing.

For a few moments, as they shared the simple pleasure of a silly joke, Jo again felt buoyed. Her misgivings about coming to the Bitterroot country receded, and she was glad she had accepted Hazel's invitation.

True, it wasn't even four in the afternoon, and she felt bone-weary from their hike. However, it was a good, satisfying kind of weary. Tonight she would enjoy the deep sleep that exertion demanded. It was nice to fall asleep quickly without memories of Ned Wilson playing over and over in her mind like a videotape she couldn't turn off.

"Seriously," Hazel qualified, crumbling bark to kindle her fire, "we dames of the ancient regime don't mind providing you hot little numbers with some male recreation. Not to be confused with *pro-creation.*"

"Besides," Dottie put in, "we like ogling the hunks, too. Old women still *think* like young ones."

"But this is not a cruise," Hazel warned. "It's the Mountain Gals Rendezvous. Mainly you came up here to work on your confidence, not to expand your sex life."

Expand, Jo thought wryly. That implies I have one in the first place. Right now my cup runneth under.

Despite her motherly warning, however, Hazel aimed a sly glance at Jo—or so it appeared to Jo.

"On the other hand," Hazel tacked on, "*romance* can bloom anywhere, even in the wild. In that case, go with the flow."

If she thinks Nick Kramer cares about romance, Jo thought, then Hazel definitely had a blind spot where male motives were involved. Maybe because the widow never got back into the romance game after her husband was killed in a car accident.

Perhaps Hazel had simply forgotten, or never really learned, about predatory men like Ned Wilson. Nick Kramer, too, had "babe bagger" stamped all over his handsome, smoldering features. And she had no plans to end up as one more trophy on his crowded shelf.

Jo had no problem with men exuding confidence, even a little aggression at times. But Nick's manner struck her as threatening. Maybe guys who put out fires for a living sometimes believed they were therefore experts at *starting* them, too. No doubt he'd had plenty of practice at kindling heat.

For a moment, without her conscious permission, the screen of her mind flashed torrid images of Nick and her, and heat stirred in her loins.

"…you don't cook it in the open flames," Hazel was explaining when Jo refocussed. "No flames, you bake it on the coals, wrapped in a layer of green leaves."

"Squeeze some wild onion juice on it first," Stella advised. "They grow all around this area."

While Dottie finished her demonstration, Stella went into the older women's cabin. She emerged moments later flourishing a few bottles of white Zinfandel wine.

"Rustic doesn't mean barbaric," she announced. "These will be chilling nearby in the brook."

Jo, drifting in and out of her own thoughts, finished cleaning her pile of fish, finding the task unpleasant but hardly the ordeal Kayla made it out to be. As she wrapped the trout in leaves and carried them to Hazel, she couldn't shake the memory of her earlier encounter with Nick down at the river.

Maybe you should see a shrink to deal with this man-hating thing of yours.

At the memory of his taunt, anger knotted her insides. Not only was he in love with himself, he obviously liked playing the expert in female psychology.

"Something biting at you, hon?" Hazel inquired

innocently as Jo deposited her catch near the crackling fire.

Jo glanced into Hazel's Prussian-blue eyes. Despite the woman's grandmotherly chignon and petite frame, however, Jo was not fooled. This old gal could follow you into a revolving door and come out ahead.

"Nothing biting but flies," Jo fibbed.

But in truth, anticipation of Nick Kramer's arrival made her feel as if she was descending too fast on a long elevator ride. He was putting the moves on her, no question, and the physical hunger within her was sharpened, for he was undeniably attractive. At an animal level.

The same hunger she had felt when Professor Ned Wilson first stroked her arm during a conference in his office.

The same, she repeated mentally. This isn't just déjà vu. You're in danger of splitting on the same hard rock you hit before. Mess around with this smoke jumper and you will get burned.

She could not prove he was just a moral copy of Ned. But her every instinct told her both of them were born to take their pleasure, then cut and run.

She knew women who felt and acted that way, too, and she didn't condemn such an attitude when both partners were up-front about it. But better loneliness, she decided, than to repeat the laceration of her heart, the long, agonizing nights of tears and despair, the numbing sense of betrayal and worthlessness.

"Pardon me?" Jo said, for Hazel had just said something to her.

"I said if you looked any lower, you'd be walking on your bottom lip. You were having fun a few minutes ago. S'matter? Thinking about that sleazebag professor again?"

"It's that obvious, huh?"

"Plain as bedbugs on a clean sheet. Look, just forget that jerk. And be dang glad you are not his wife. She's the real victim of his philandering. And so are his kids."

Jo nodded, swiping some loose strands of hair from her eyes. She managed a genuine smile. "You're right."

"I usually am," Hazel observed drolly. "How could I be so smart *and* so damn good-looking? The total package, babycakes."

The two women laughed. Just then, however, Dottie called, "Here comes the invasion!"

Jo glanced across the camp clearing and felt her pulse quicken when she spotted Nick Kramer.

"All those fish crowding the river today," Dottie remarked to Nick. "Is that a bad sign as to the fire danger?"

Nick, like Jo, had finished eating. The two of them sat in the grass cross-legged, not exactly together but uncomfortably close, in Jo's opinion, sipping wine from paper cups.

"Right now," Nick replied to Dottie's question,

"all area fires are reported under control if not fully contained. But so far the conditions haven't improved as we thought they would. I'm not predicting any trouble for Crying Horse Canyon. Things could get a little hairy around here, though, if we get airborne sparks."

Jo had noticed how all the other firefighters acted as if Nick had dibs on her. They had formed little groups around all of them, with Kayla the biggest draw of all.

But Kayla only toyed with her admirers, flitting from male to male like a bee sampling different nectars, her eyes ever fixed on Nick. Jo steeled herself when Kayla, making a show of brushing leaves off the taut seat of her blue jeans, crossed to join her and Nick.

"Jo's momma was Miss Montana, you know that, Nick?" Kayla greeted them.

Her tone, Jo thought, was saying, *Can you believe that? How could a kennel-registered breed produce such a common mutt?*

"Well, then, the odds are good her mother's not a blonde," Nick said, not a hint of malice in his tone.

"Huh?" Kayla, thrown off her game, was suddenly wary.

Nick shrugged, looking at Jo and not Kayla. "What I mean is, society gives blondes all the publicity, they have more fun, all that. But I've read that it's brunettes who actually win most beauty pageants."

"All right. They might win the pageants, but we have all the fun," Kayla conceded, fluffing her hair.

Nick laughed. "Just the facts, ma'am, just the facts."

"How 'bout you?" Kayla pressed the issue. "Personal preference, I mean. Blondes or brunettes?"

"Definitely brunettes," he replied, which left Kayla deflated but not defeated.

It startled Jo, too.

She had steeled herself for more unfair comparisons with her mother. But Nick's surprise comment had thrown Kayla over a fence.

It doesn't mean Nick's taking my side, Jo mused. He's just getting a dig in at Kayla. He didn't seem nearly as captivated by her as some of his crew did. Maybe I've sold him a little short.

Unless, warned a cautious, protective inner voice, he's simply an accomplished master at seduction. Perhaps he's like a stalking lion, crafty by instinct. Perhaps he's learned that playing hard to get works with some women and he's just using you to ignite Kayla. After all, Kayla appeared unfazed by his ungallant remarks just now. In fact, she seemed all the more determined.

Kayla was on the verge of trying another tack when Hazel, observant as a circling hawk, joined them.

"Kayla, dear, you're ignoring our other guests," the cattle queen said diplomatically. "After all, you're one of the main reasons they're here. And who could blame them, you little Texas bombshell? Now don't disappoint your admirers. Mingle, mingle, disperse your considerable charms so all may enjoy.''

Hazel's blandishments worked. Kayla smiled at the flattery and left, and Hazel turned to the taciturn couple.

"There's one more bottle of wine cooling in the brook. Would you mind going to fetch it, Jo?''

"I'll go, Hazel,'' Nick said quickly, rising lithely to his feet.

"No, you're our guest,'' Jo said. "I'll go.''

He extended a hand to help her up.

Jo knew Hazel watched them, her eyes narrowing with pleasure.

A tactful refusal was needed, but Jo couldn't think of one. So she took his hand, marveling at his easy strength as he tugged her effortlessly up.

"It's in that little clutch of boulders right past the pump,'' Hazel added. "Same place you go to get the drinking water, Jo.''

Jo could've sworn that a look passed between Hazel and Nick, and that a smile flitted over his lips but didn't quite land.

Don't be ridiculous, she chided herself as Nick adjusted his long-legged pace to hers along the looping, descending path. Even if Hazel was playing Cupid, she certainly wasn't conspiring with Nick. How could she be? But the delusion was understandable viewed through the lens of Ned Wilson's dishonesty and the damage it caused her.

"Like it up here?" Nick asked, his tone friendly and easy.

"It's beautiful here. I don't even mind all the work," Jo replied matter-of-factly.

He seemed determined, however, to regain her favor after their little altercation earlier.

"Hazel mentioned yesterday that you're a teacher," he ventured. "What subject?"

"Music," she answered hesitantly. She feigned great interest in the aspens and spruces, hazed in the spun gold of the westering sun.

"What instruments do you play?"

"Piano and guitar." She peeked at him. He seemed genuinely interested and sincere, which downright terrified her. A smug, narcissistic jerk she could toss on his rear. A downright nice guy might actually get under her skin and really hurt her. "I especially like the guitar. Mostly classical and flamenco."

"I don't have a musical bone in my body," he confessed as they crossed the stone footbridge. "I don't even sing in the shower. But I've heard the guitar is the easiest instrument in the world to play badly, the hardest in the world to play well."

He was right, and this unexpected comment surprised and impressed her. But instead of warming up to him, she felt a quick flood of caution. There might be no limits to the sheer depths of his smoothness. She really had to be careful. He could be one of those guys who had a remark to suit every taste, as if memorized from flash cards. Until she knew better, she would do well to suspect he was up to something. The handsome spider might just be reeling in his fly…and frankly, if she hadn't still been feeling the wounds from Ned, maybe she'd even let herself be reeled in. No doubt Nick Kramer took great care to please a woman in bed.

"Here, I'll get it," he offered when she started to clamber down the steep bank of the bubbling brook. The wine bottle was visible from above, neck protruding fron an encirclement of half-submerged rocks.

She opened her mouth to demur, but in moments the lithe, agile smoke jumper had grabbed the bottle and climbed back up again. She couldn't help noticing the swelling of muscles in his back and shoulders as he bent down to grasp the bottle.

"Candy's dandy, but liquor's quicker," he quipped as he handed her the wine.

He'd used his contracted version of the old Ogden Nash quote quite harmlessly, she realized later when she recalled her walk with him. But at the moment, in her defensive mood, something about it and Nick's tone as he delivered it again reminded her of Ned.

She gave him a wary stare.

"Don't tell me I just grew horns again," he groaned. "I've seen wild fillies less skittish than you."

"I'm not some filly for you to corral," she returned.

His eyes darkened with anger. "You take one look at a guy," he snapped, "and you know everything about him, right? Well, guess what—you don't know jack.''

"So what do you think I am?" she lashed back. "A Forest Service camp follower? A smoke-jumper groupie? Just because I'm here doesn't mean you have to hit on me. Or that I have to succumb."

"Hit on…?" His handsome features tightened. "For God's sake," he said disgustedly. "Are you a ball-breaker by nature, or is it just me you despise?"

It wasn't his words that suddenly intensified her anger like flames in a gust—it was his tone. In fact, he had a real knack for using his tone with the subtle force of raised eyebrows. A trait, unfortunately, that instantly reminded her yet again of Ned Wilson.

Ned, too, had a dry, subtle sense of humor—and absolutely no sense of honor. It wasn't fair to tar Nick with the same brush, but she couldn't help wondering—did Nick also share Ned's talent for deceit?

She eyed him with cool distaste.

"It's just you I despise," she flung back at him, forgetting to lower her voice as they approached the summit campground.

"Yeah, well, you know what?" Nick tapped his left temple. "You're free to hate my guts all you want. But I think you've left some of your groceries at the market. You're certifiable, lady."

"Right, I agree! I must be nuts to be alone with you."

Unfortunately for both of them, she was wrong about one point—they were no longer alone. In fact, this last, heated exchange was once again heard by everyone in the camp.

The rest burst into spontaneous cheers and applause, and Jo felt her cheeks heat with embarrassment.

"Oh, yeah, she *wants* you, Nick," one of the smoke jumpers yelled out, and Nick, too, flushed to his earlobes.

"Point, set, match!" hollered another.

And it was Hazel alone, Jo noticed, who was not enjoying a good laugh. Instead, she was only smiling.

The crafty, knowing smile of a master manipulator.

Six

Thanks to the relentless schedule that her two cronies planned, Jo had little time to brood over the latest embarrassment Nick Kramer had caused her. Instead, she and her companions were subjected to a crash course in wilderness skills.

It was Hazel and Dottie who gave the initial lessons in proper river rafting. They had packed along two military-surplus canvas-and-rubber rafts.

Now both crafts were afloat in a calm pool above the churning white-water rapids of "the chute"—a stretch of the Stony Rapids River that descended a steep slope to the canyon floor. The falls were well out of sight from this point, but Jo could hear the water hissing and brawling in the distance, a constant but muted roar.

"Kayla!" Dottie shouted at the younger woman, shaking her head in exasperation. "Hon, what in plu-perfect hell are you doing? We said paddle east, not west."

Kayla pouted. "Sorry, Aunt Dottie. Isn't east your right hand, west your left?"

"Only if you're facing north," Hazel explained with a martyr's patience.

"No wonder we were going in circles," Bonnie muttered in Jo's ear while Kayla corrected her stroke. "She's so dizzy, it seemed like a straight line to her."

Jo hardly noticed. She could see the spray from the falls beyond making little rainbows in the bright afternoon sunlight. The only ominous sight was the smoke from the nearby fires that sometimes drifted over the sun like a thick, dark filter.

"The chute is all bark and very little bite," Hazel scoffed. "It's rated one of the easier rafting sites in the state, or we wouldn't send you greenhorns through it at the end of the ten days. I'd ride it myself if my hinges weren't a bit too rusted. I quit running the river about five years ago."

"You'll thank us after you take the plunge," Dottie assured them. "It's more fun than the best roller coaster you've ever been on. You'll be proud you did it and ready to do it again. Wait and see."

Jo noticed the black smoke on the ridge beyond, and she was plagued by the same question that had gnawed at her off and on since yesterday: was she treating Nick Kramer unfairly?

Are you a ball-breaker by nature, or is it just me you despise?

Just you, she had told him in the heat of anger.

But then again, maybe all that heat had not been anger. Maybe it was something else, something more needful and demanding that she was trying to deny. It was hard to pretend that Nick wasn't an exciting and sexy man.

If I'm really so glad to be rid of him, she admitted in candor, then why is he on my mind so much?

Indeed, she might just as well be with him.

Kayla studied Jo's preoccupied face. Despite her "dumb blonde" act, the pretty Texan seemed uncanny at sensing thoughts.

She said something, but lost in her reverie, Jo didn't hear her.

"Pardon me?"

"Your mind is roaming, teacher," Bonnie scolded before Kayla could say anything. "We're supposed to be heading away from shore now."

"Sorry," Jo replied, hastily adjusting the stroke of her paddle. "Guess I was daydreaming."

"I'd guess more like fantasizing," Kayla said.

"About a broad-shouldered hunk with a mischievous gleam in his eye," Bonnie teased.

Kayla's mouth twisted downward in a frown.

Jo felt compelled to say something. "He's not my type. Really," she offered. "Besides, if we can't endure ten days without the comfort of a man's attention, we've got an addiction problem."

"That's right," Bonnie grunted as she helped tug the raft up onto shore. "You know, there's even a national group called Sexaholics Anonymous. Just think, a roomful of horny people all in the same room. I'm ready to join right now."

"You're just bitter, Lofton," Kayla said, out of breath. "Dottie told me about that prof who tossed you aside. But I'm not bitter. And I'm going after Nick Kramer."

Jo stared at her for a long moment. Finally she announced, "Well, you be my guest, Kayla," before she retreated toward the campsite.

"Baker One, this is Baker One Actual. Do you read me? Over."

Jason Baumgarter took his finger off the push-to-talk switch on his handheld field radio. A burst of static was followed by a reply from the fire-command center on nearby Copper Mountain.

"This is Baker One. Read you loud and clear, Hotshots. Go ahead, over."

Reluctantly Nick pushed Jo Lofton out of his thoughts and took the radio from Jason.

"Request a status report from your sector. My crew's about to go on duty. Over."

"Roger that. So far all blazes are contained. But we've got wind picking up, with little spot fires from windborn embers outside the containment perimeter. Nothing major so far. Over."

"Roger your report, Baker One."

"But don't fall asleep at the switch, guys, or we could be facing some nasty rollovers."

Nick frowned at this news, his amber-brown gaze fixed on the smoke columns to his east, near Copper Mountain. A rollover was a reburn, the sudden flaring-up of a smoldering area caused by too little moisture in the air.

"Roger that," he replied. "We'll go back down in the canyon, thin out some more green. You heard any talk yet of evacuating the campers over here? Over."

"Negative on that. Over."

"Roger. Over and out."

Nick handed the radio back to Jason, who hung it from his utility belt. All around them, firefighters were pulling on their boots and bulky equipment packs, checking their first-aid pouches and otherwise preparing to move out for a hard night's work by moonlight.

"Could be worse," said Nick's second-in-command, Tom Albers, who had overheard the radio report. "I'd ruther bust my hump on the ax than mop up the burns."

"Who wouldn't?" Nick agreed, though absently, for Jo had edged back into his thoughts. Not that she ever strayed from them very long, even though he wished she would.

Tonight it wasn't his job that weighed on Nick, but a pretty brunette with too much attitude. And he resented having her dominate his thoughts like this. Resented...and perhaps even feared.

It had been a long time since any woman had gained hold of his thoughts as she had. A long time since he had let any female get to him as she had already.

Not since Karen delivered her fateful ultimatum: *I want a guy who punches a clock and comes home every night, not some unshaven nomad who's gone for weeks at a time so we have to get reacquainted each time he comes around.*

"That Kayla's pretty hot," Tom ventured. "Likes to show off her bod. Think she's just a tease?"

Nick grinned at that, remembering a phrase one of his foster mothers reserved for "fast" women.

"Oh, I think she's been kissed in the taxi a few times," he replied.

"Huh? What taxi?"

Tom puzzled that one out while Nick went back to thinking about Karen and how his old bitter anger was still there.

If she hadn't forced him away, she might have gotten more or less what she wanted.

Hell, Nick didn't consider himself married to his job just because he was good at it. It was interesting, challenging work, good experience for a few years, and it had helped him work his way through college at UC Boulder.

But as much as he had enjoyed earning a degree in earth science, he stuck with smoke jumping because it was familiar, all he really knew how to do, in fact.

And for a kid abandoned by his parents, filled with

rage, it also provided a sense of purpose and a physical outlet for his anger.

But deep in his heart of hearts he was looking for one good reason to quit and put down roots someplace. Maybe put his degree to work teaching fulltime; he'd done some substitute teaching and enjoyed it.

One good reason…a reason like Jo Lofton, maybe. Except that she had Karen stamped all over her. Cold, autocratic, willful, unbending. Not to mention gorgeous and sexy.

Forget it, his inner voice urged. That woman will do the hurt dance on you if you don't put her out of your plans.

Reflect, deflect and move on, he told himself harshly.

Jason Baumgarter came over to join Tom and Nick.

"What the hell's bugging you?" he demanded, studying Nick's preoccupied frown. "Got angst in your pants, boss?"

"Nah, I'm ready to go," Nick forced himself to say, shaking off his pensive mood.

"You know what I just realized?" Tom announced.

"Share your wisdom with us, Einstein," Jason grunted.

"Crying Horse Canyon," he said, "is laid out almost exactly like South Canyon in Colorado."

Nick said nothing, feeling ice encase his spine as he realized Tom was right. A sudden inversion during

the South Canyon fire in '94 had killed fourteen Hotshots—and left Tom's older brother, a smoke jumper,
permanently disabled.

"Bad luck to mention bad fires," he reminded his
friend. "Let's hit the trail, gents, earn that big
money."

All during the hike to the canyon floor, however,
the screen of Nick's mind was filled with the pleasant
image of Jo Lofton, in various stages of dress and
undress. Yet, her defiant words dug at him like a stone
in his boot: *Just because I'm here doesn't mean you
have to hit on me. Or that I have to succumb.*

Seven

Early in her fourth morning in the Bitterroot National Forest, Jo was up before sunrise to haul cooking and drinking water.

Summer was on the wane, and at this altitude the morning air was crisp. In the dull, leaden light of dawn she could see her breath forming little ghost puffs. Shivering a bit, her chin tucked in against the chill, she hurried down the meanders of the hiking path, water container in hand.

Nothing disturbed the pristine silence except the rising shrill of the dawn chorus. She paused, startled into awareness of a beautiful red fox just ahead, peering at her from the opening of its den. The pointy face retreated into the ground at her next step.

Jo was perhaps twenty feet from the stone foot-bridge when she heard male voices, several of them, approaching her from the opposite direction.

Oh, great timing, Lofton, she berated herself. Guess who's getting off work? And it sure as heck looks like you timed things so you'd meet them, doesn't it?

Meet *him*.

For a few moments, desperately wishing she could just duck into a hole the way that fox did, Jo considered fleeing back to camp. She just might have time to—

Just then Nick Kramer hiked onto the bridge, spotted her, and it was too late.

The other Hotshots crowded onto the bridge and noticed her, too.

"Hey, there's your new sparring partner, Nick!" called out a guy carrying a portable radio transceiver.

Jo searched her memory a second and recalled his name was Jason. One of the guys most attentive to Kayla.

"No wonder our fearless leader prac'ly double-timed us back. He's got an appointment to keep," Jason added.

Jo felt heat in her face as the guys all released a racket of whistles and harmless risqué teasing. They *did* assume, just as she'd feared, that she'd deliberately planned this meeting. No doubt assumed Nick had, too.

"Knock it off, you morons," Nick snapped, or

tried to—in his own embarrassment, his command sounded lame and halfhearted.

"C'mon, boys," another piped up, "we're cramping Romeo's style. Let's leave these lovebirds alone."

Somebody made loud kissing noises. To Jo's further chagrin, Nick did peel off from his team of smoke jumpers as they filed past Jo, heading back to their camp. Guys winked at her as they passed. One even greeted her suggestively: "Wanna go skinny-dippin', muffin?"

"Hope you don't mind," Nick said to Jo as the guys moved off.

"Mind what?" she retorted, starting across the bridge toward the pump. "The teasing, you mean? I've walked past construction sites and gotten worse."

"No, I mean, mind if I walk back with you."

Once again a diplomatic refusal was needed, but as usual she could not think of one.

He stood at the far end of the bridge, and she had to squeeze around him to get at the pump.

At the moment he hardly made an impressive picture, she thought silently. The odor of dried sweat was obvious, as was the rumpled, soiled condition of his clothing.

But fairness made her admit that, after all, he'd spent the past twelve hours doing hard physical work, not hunched over a computer. And when she brushed past him, she realized she liked the wild, exciting, distinctly masculine smell of him. She even imagined she could feel his animal warmth—unless the heat she felt was her own sexual response to his nearness.

"The only time I've seen a woman as cold as you are to me is when she'd been kicked. Did someone kick you, girl?"

The question caught her off guard. He knew it, too. She saw how he'd read her sharp intake of breath.

"L-look," she said haltingly, "I don't want to spar with you anymore. I just came on this trip to be alone. If it's a woman you're after, Kayla's more than ready for you, trust me."

"You didn't answer my question." His gaze held hers like a magnet.

She took a deep, reviving breath. "I'm not looking for a relationship, if that's what you're after."

"Why?" he demanded in that sexy groan of a voice he had.

Caught like a fly in a web, she struggled and struggled to get away from his pull, but it was useless. His hold was too strong. Finally she gave him an inch. Staring at him, knowing there was hurt in her eyes, she whispered, "Because I was kicked."

One of the threads from his web seemed to wrap around her heart at that moment.

He didn't gloat over his triumph. He didn't move or change expression. But the honesty was in his eyes. For the first time, she even wondered if he'd been kicked, too.

It was obvious why they couldn't get along, she

thought. Their defense mechanisms were making both of them lash out.

She struggled to hold the opening of the water container up close to the spout of the pump.

This time when Nick offered to help, she let him.

When the container was full, she knew she had to break the uncomfortable silence between them. Because the silence was speaking much too loudly.

"Look," she offered in an even tone, "there's no law against raging hormones, but I didn't come up here with sex high on my agenda."

"And I did, I suppose? That's why I'm wearing this Armani dinner jacket and the Gucci loafers?"

Thin-lipped and severely handsome in his sudden anger, he laughed harshly.

She bristled. Still hoping to take charge, she said, "Look, why can't we just be friends?"

She stood facing him, the container held between them. He suddenly put it on the bridge and moved closer. She took a reflexive step backward, but the cement foundation of the pump stopped her.

"What are you doing?" she protested.

"I don't think you and I are ever going to be friends," he said, so close now she could feel his breath on her face, intimately warm. His amber-brown eyes seemed to burn with a wild, carnal ardor that did indeed excite her, a tight, hot tickle low in her belly, as if her loins were toaster coils suddenly heating up.

"Why n-not?" she stammered, ready to flee like a frightened hare.

"Because this is always going to get in the way," he murmured.

She didn't dare look at him. She knew if she did, she would fall prey to the hunger inside her, a ferocious emptiness that suddenly sprang to life like the fires he so valiantly fought.

A second ticked by. A long, interminable second. He didn't move. She didn't move.

If she wanted the moment to end, all she had to do was sidestep him and go about her business. There was no need to look at him, no need to address him. He was bigger than her by far, but she instinctively sensed invitation, not threat, in his proximity.

One little step aside and the moment would shatter like broken glass. She could walk across the pieces and never look back.

Instead, she made the fatal error.

She looked at him.

Her gaze locked with his and the craziness inside her took over. Invitation accepted.

His mouth came down on hers, the kiss at first gentle and enticing. She melted into it. Since Ned, no one had touched her, kissed her, seduced her. Unable to admit it until now, she realized the emptiness gnawed inside her, and Nick seemed the only one who could fill it.

Sensing her surrender, he wrapped his strong arms around her and effortlessly pulled her to him.

Like her, he became greedier. His mouth turned hard and demanding. He easily parted her lips, and she shocked herself by responding, instead of resisting. Moaning, she accepted his exploring tongue; wantonly, almost drugged by his touch and his thick male scent, she pressed her body hard into his. Wanting. Needing. The need ran through her like a drug.

What are you doing? a horrified inner voice demanded, but she couldn't stop herself.

He took her head in both hands and deepened the kiss. His thrusting tongue licked fire all through her. Her own hands curled into balls and nestled against the sheet of the muscle on his chest. Intoxicated, she pressed even more into him, the rock between his loins delicious against her belly.

"Hey, you two, get a room!"

At the unexpected sound of Kayla's voice, Jo nearly cried out.

Oh, God, no!

She twisted loose from Nick's arms, flushing even warmer, if that was possible.

"If we can't endure ten days without the comfort of a man's attention," Kayla said, flinging Jo's words back at her, "we've got an addiction problem."

She stood halfway out on the bridge, haughty and accusatory. Worse, Jo couldn't muster enough indignation to fight back—she felt like a sneaking, two-faced hypocrite.

"We've got a spying problem, too," Jo finally managed to retort. Nick's searing kiss had left her heart pounding like fists on a drum, her throat so constricted she could barely find her voice. And Kayla must have noticed it.

"Spying schmying." Kayla rubbed it in spitefully. "I think this proves which one of us is man-hungry."

Kayla's green gaze shifted to Nick. "She plays hard to get, and you fall for it. But how long did it take your 'nice girl' to rub up against you like a cat? Just remember, Nick—she's pulled her lah-de-dah act on plenty of guys before you. I'd be very, very careful to practice safe sex with her."

On that spiteful and triumphant note, Kayla spun gracefully around and flounced off.

"Look," Nick began awkwardly, "I didn't know she was here—"

"Please just leave me alone," Jo cut him off coldly. Anger and mortification—along with a good dose of self-loathing—all warred within her.

"Please, I—"

"Why did you have to do that?" she again cut him off.

"You didn't seem to mind until Kayla piped up."

"Wrong! You…you caught me off guard, is all. I would've stopped you after I—after—"

"After you cooled down a little? You sure got plenty warm all of a sudden."

"I meant to say after I caught my breath!" Jo insisted, pushing him aside and hurrying onto the bridge.

"Yeah, hot and breathless, that describes you, all right," Nick teased even as she escaped in mortified anger. "That's exactly how I'm going to remember you, sweetheart."

Despite her immediate relief after fleeing from Nick Kramer, Jo quickly realized she was a woman without sanctuary. The moment she returned to camp, she felt Kayla's smug eyes tracking her everywhere like video security.

It still hadn't quite registered with Jo; not only had she responded eagerly to Nick's advance, she had proved Kayla right. Or so it certainly appeared. But Jo still fooled herself that she was the victim of circumstances and false impressions.

He *did* cut me off in midbreath, she assured herself. My response was confused, delayed, my body didn't have my mind's permission. He caught me completely by surprise.

"Randy" is just another word for young and healthy, she thought.

Hazel's voice cut into her unpleasant thoughts. "Good morning, sourpuss. What's the matter?"

"Morning, Hazel," Jo replied tersely. She was busy filling the smaller water jug used for cooking. "I'm doing just fine."

Hazel gave that reply a skeptical snort.

"Kayla's up and dressed," Hazel remarked with exaggerated innocence as she put coffee water on to boil. "And looking smug as the cat that tortured the canary before he ate it. Don't tell me you two've locked horns already this morning with the birds barely awake."

"Kayla? I didn't notice," Jo replied.

Dottie, still brushing her thick white hair, emerged from the cabin, her nose sampling the air.

"Where's the coffee?" she demanded. "There's no life possible without caffeine."

"Oh, Jo's got us all behind schedule," Hazel teased. "A certain Hotshot has got her all discombobulated."

Anger spiked Jo's pulse.

"You don't help any," she said, exasperated. "I've got a strong hunch you're playing Cupid again, Hazel."

Hazel winked at Dottie.

"Plead guilty," the cattle baroness replied, "and you avoid the jury."

"Yes," Jo fumed, "but what about that tangled web we weave, et cetera?"

Her accusing gaze happened to land on Dottie.

"Don't look at me," Dottie protested in her acquired Texas twang. "I've got no dog in this fight. As for Cupid, how comes he's always naked, anyhow?"

Despite her anger and embarrassment, Jo couldn't help laughing at both sly old gals and their shenanigans. They're just girls, too, Jo realized, still plotting schoolgirl pranks and playing "guess who's got a boyfriend."

Jo's mood lightened even though the tension between her and Kayla persisted throughout another busy day in the wilderness.

Hazel made it all fun, but Jo's mind kept drifting back to that searing kiss. Just the momentary thought of it was enough to set her pulse exploding in her ears, drowning out Hazel.

"Now remember," Hazel wrapped up her remarks that evening, "tomorrow night we're all going to drive two miles away from camp, then break up into teams. Each of the younger gals has to guide the way back to camp using the night sky and the reference points I've already pointed out. Got it?"

"Got it," Bonnie and Kayla said.

But Jo didn't answer with the rest. She found herself transported as sleepiness gradually weighed on her eyelids and the day's exertions left a pleasant ache in muscles she hardly ever used. Now and then, however, she returned to the present and saw Kayla staring at her, resentful and smugly superior.

Don't worry, Jo fumed silently. From now on I mean it, Nick Kramer is all yours. So put away your voodoo spells.

But his words echoed in her unwilled memory, exciting and forbidden, a promise of much more to come: *Because this is always going to get in the way.*

Eight

"**D**on't forget," Dottie shouted over the steady brawling of the nearby rapids, "you never fight the current. Just let it shoot you up the middle. If you get confused, disoriented, turned around or even tossed into the river, do not panic. Always let the current take you. It follows the path of least resistance."

"Do not panic," Bonnie repeated, trying to sound lighthearted but betrayed by her nervousness. "After all, the rocks only hurt if you actually hit them."

"Oh, don't be such a fraidy-cat," Hazel teased, floating alongside them in the other raft. "You're all strong swimmers, and besides, you're wearing life vests."

Jo felt nervous anticipation crowding other

thoughts from her mind, thoughts that mostly tended toward Nick Kramer and his smoldering, no pun intended, good looks. The kiss on the bridge had played out over and over in her dreams last night, and despite the high-altitude chill after dark, she was forced to throw off the top blanket.

You need challenges like this, she assured herself as the roar of the approaching rapids really began to drown out other sounds.

Nothing focused the mind like fear.

"Oh, how this aching body misses the feel of a black knit dress," Kayla wailed beside her, barely audible above the river racket.

At least it wasn't another snide comment about Nick, Jo thought gratefully. So far their mutual dependence had pushed all hostilites onto a back burner.

"Ride 'em, cowgirls!" Hazel shouted in front of them as the first raft suddenly dipped, then shot out of the water when the frothing rapids gained a purchase. "Up the middle, ladies!" she reminded them, and then Jo lost sight of the lead raft as their own craft suddenly plunged into a curtain of misting, roaring foam.

"I wanna go home!" Bonnie wailed just before the rapids drowned out all conversation.

But it turned out they could indeed trust the current. It kept them safely in the middle, and they only needed to occasionally fend off a boulder that came too close, pushing against it with their paddles.

In mere moments, their distressed cries turned into

shouts of pure, astonished fun as this crazy, bobbing thrill ride picked up dizzying speed and made all of them feel like little kids riding the Tilt-A-Whirl at the county fair.

All too soon, however, the ride was over, and they floated quietly in the wide pool, all four talking at once and insisting on running the course again.

"Told you," Hazel gloated as the women trekked back upriver, carrying the light rafts between them by rope handles. "See how much fun you miss by acting like city sissies?"

In the adrenaline rush, Nick Kramer was finally pushed from Jo's thoughts, but when they arrived back at camp late that afternoon and Hazel made a mysterious disappearance, Jo couldn't help but feel uneasy. It didn't do not to watch that matriarchal matchmaker. Hazel was usually up to no good, and Jo was convinced she was now the target of the woman's schemes.

Hazel had learned, when the smoke jumpers stopped by for supper two days earlier, that tonight they would be off duty. And she had made plans then to ensure that Jo would "bump into" Nick Kramer later tonight, during the star-navigating exercise.

First, however, she had a certain motherly duty to attend to. After all, if she was going to cross Jo's path with Nick's, she needed to peer a little closer into Nick's heart. Hazel trusted her first impressions, and instinct told her Nick was a "keeper."

Nonetheless, Jo had recently sailed through rough romantic waters, and Hazel had no desire to plunge her vulnerable friend into a whirlpool of additional heartache.

She waited until late that afternoon, when the girls were helping with supper and the smoke jumpers were likely to be awake after their previous night's labors. Then Hazel slipped quietly away to visit the men's camp, which was located about two hundred yards below the cabins on Bridger's Summit.

"Getcher britches on, boys!" she called out as she approached their circle of one-man tents. "Female approaching camp!"

In fact, a few of the firefighters were barely dressed, and Hazel discreetly ogled some sloping pecs as her eye quickly rushed over the camp, looking for Nick. She spotted him immediately, shaving in front of a metal mirror that had been nailed to a tree.

"Hazel," he greeted her cheerfully, scraping some bristle off one side of his strong-jutting jaw. "Excuse us if we're not ready for company. What brings you to our neck of the woods?"

"I'm just curious about something," she replied, glancing around to make sure none of the lounging men was close enough to overhear.

"Oh, yeah? What?"

"What's your honest opinion of Jo?"

"Jo?" he repeated.

"We've established her name," Hazel said. "Now tell me what you think of her."

Nick's eyes cut from the mirror to Hazel's face, then back to the mirror. He angled the razor up under his nose and said cautiously, "Who wants to know?"

"I'm the one asking, aren't I? Just spit it out, big boy. I won't share it with her."

"Well…she's damn good-looking," he essayed, obviously holding back. "Great face, great body."

"All right, for a man that's a typical start. But let's get past the cattle auction. What else do you think of her?"

"Not so quick," he resisted. "What's she think of me?"

"Not too much, evidently."

Hazel's bluntness was deliberate, and just as she'd hoped, her candor triggered his own.

"Well, since you insist on knowing, the feeling is mutual," Nick retorted, his voice revealing resentment. "She's the pouty-princess type, thinks her pedestal is mighty high. Likes to stamp her foot and lay down all the rules, push a guy around for the power rush. I've had it up to here with women who deliver ultimatums."

He almost said more, Hazel could tell, but he suddenly shut up.

Still, sunlight is the best disinfectant, thought a jubilant Hazel, and his brief comments just now threw open casements of illumination. Just like Jo, he'd obviously been hurt in love, and also like her, he was confusing the person who hurt him with all members of the opposite sex. A common mistake, but also a tragic one.

Both these kids, Hazel marveled, are proud and sensitive, and ironically, have much more in common than they suspected. They were both also emotionally defensive, and neither was the enemy the other suspected.

However, she also realized they couldn't simply be told these things. The heart was no friend of logic. They'd have to learn it the tough way in the school of romantic hard knocks.

"Nick, have you heard the expression 'A burned baby fears the fire'?"

His eyes met Hazel's again.

"Sure I have. But don't forget," he joked, "I'm trained to see how close I can get to the fire without being burned."

"Nobody yet has fireproofed himself against romantic burns."

"Tell me about it," he admitted. Then he added, "So was Jo burned quite recently? I wondered."

Hazel nodded without going into the details. "And it's not just that. I've known Jo for a long time now. She's had to work harder than most girls to be taken as her own person. Sometimes our parents cast a long shadow over us without meaning to."

For a moment, as he patted shaving cream off his face with a towel, Nick frowned. "Sometimes they cast no shadow at all, and that's worse."

"I take your meaning." Hazel nodded again. "But

Jo's got a problem with the former Miss Montana. A tall, gregarious, very leggy Miss Montana,'' she clarified. ''One who modeled professionally and is still quite a celebrity in our little town. Ranks right up there with our only rodeo champ, AJ Clayburn.''

Nick mulled this awhile, then nodded.

''Maybe,'' Hazel hinted, ''if you two could get a little time to yourselves, you might work some of these knots.''

Nick saw the canny gleam in her Prussian-blue eyes, and a little conspiratorial smile twitched at his lips.

''Might be we could,'' he agreed. ''But she sure hasn't made me feel welcome to come visiting.''

''So what? A faint heart never won a fair lady, buckaroo. Where d'you plan on being tonight, say, around eight o'clock? Maybe...someplace a little more private than this?''

Nick did a good job of playing along.

''Sometimes, on nights off like this, I like to go over to Wendigo Lake just to get some time alone. You know where it is?''

Hazel nodded, realizing the place would be perfect for her matchmaking efforts. Rustic and romantic, encircled by spruce and pine, Wendigo Lake was within sight of Bridger's Summit—she could easily excuse herself at that point, knowing Jo could not possibly get lost from there.

''Moon's in the full phase now,'' Nick added. ''Light enough I can do a little fishing off that old dock on the south shore. You know the one I mean, don't you?''

"Why don't you stroll over that way this evening?'' Hazel suggested casually. "Maybe some company will show up. Maybe not. At this point, no guarantees.''

"All right, I will. If nobody shows up, fine, I'll get in some fishing. Bass bite in moonlight.''

But despite all her encouragement, Hazel felt compelled to add a clear caveat before she returned to camp.

"Don't get me wrong, Nick. Jo is much tougher than she thinks she is, and I've always trusted her judgment. She's fully capable of making her own decisions. But as her friend, who's more or less responsible for her up here, I'd hate to see some guy hurt her by sailing under false colors. She's had too much of that already.''

"I read you loud and clear, Hazel. Don't worry. I'm not the feed-'em-a-line-of-bull type.''

"That's my hunch about you, too,'' the cattle queen pronounced.

But as she returned to her own camp, she had to admit it: the fate of this potential romance was just too hard to call.

Even if Nick was not the bad sort at all, she could not entirely discount his hint about an unhappy childhood. For reasons beyond his control he might not have it together emotionally—lots of guys in rugged, macho jobs were too emotionally bottled up inside, one reason they sought jobs that were conducive to the loner and his need to avoid too much society. She'd seen it in many of the cowboys she'd hired over the years.

Jo needed a man, sure, but one who was mature and responsible. There were plenty of men with strong backs and weak characters.

For Jo's sake, and for the sake of Mystery Valley's future, Hazel would take the gamble.

Nine

Supper was cooking by the time Hazel returned to the cabins, and the girls were busy playing doubles badminton.

Jo, however, had missed several easy shots, forcing her partner, Bonnie, to take most of the swings at the shuttlecock.

"Jeez oh Pete, Lofton!" Bonnie scolded her good-naturedly. "I've seen better form toppling a windmill! Building castles in our mind, are we?"

"Castles? A honeymoon suite, more likely," Kayla suggested. "Or maybe just a double sleeping bag that smells of wood smoke and the last girl's cheap perfume."

"Cool it, mighty mouth," Stella admonished.

"You'd know something about cheap perfume, since you've got our camp smelling like Eau de Biker."

Ignoring the fracas, Jo gave the shuttlecock a mighty swat, spiking it, and Kayla had to leap aside, almost tripping over her own feet.

"Sweetheart," Kayla said coolly, "you might want to put your glasses on. I know Miss Montana can't wear glasses, but then again, you're not Miss Montana, are you?"

Jo had been eating Kayla's snide comments, off and on, all day long. This time, however, the "Texas tart" had gone too far.

She threw down her racket and placed her fists on her hips, ready to unload on Kayla.

Stella quickly intervened. "Oh, who are you trying to kid, Kayla? You're ragging on Jo because Nick Kramer obviously prefers her over you."

By this time their voices had risen high enough to engage the attention of the other women.

"Quit the catfighting," Dottie called over to them.

But she spoke absently.

Like Hazel, she was distracted by something going on over at the adjacent ridge.

Jo followed their gazes and saw a new pall of gray-black smoke rising into the sky. Flames licked upward, fueled by the brisk breeze.

"That's a new fire," Bonnie said behind her. "It wasn't burning earlier today."

"Yeah, same thing I was thinking."

Even as they watched, a twin-engine transport

plane swept overhead. Smoke jumpers hurled out of the fuselage, their parachutes opening gauze-white against the sky.

Jo couldn't help admiring the men's obvious skill, for their drop zone was tiny and the wind was picking up. Nonetheless, they landed with precision on a lower slope and quickly began moving up to intercept and contain the outbreak.

What a way to pay the bills, she thought.

"Is that Nick Kramer's team?" Bonnie wondered out loud. "They sure haven't got much room to operate on that steep ridge."

Hazel, also busy watching the firefighters in action, turned to tell them that Nick's team had the day off. But spying the sudden look of concern on Jo's face, Hazel decided to keep mum.

After all, she reasoned, holding something back wasn't the same as telling a fib.

Supper was finished, the sun had finally gone down in a copper blaze, and the women were waiting for the moon and stars to glow a little more brightly before they set out for their various drop points. Hazel had tuned the radio to the local station out of Bighorn Creek for the evening news broadcast.

"Turning to fire news in the Bitterroot country," said the announcer, "we have a late report, just in, that two smoke jumpers were injured, one seriously, while escaping from a sudden firewall on Bent's Ridge."

"That's the next ridge over!" Dottie exclaimed. "Must be the guys we saw jumping a little while ago."

"One man was treated on the scene for minor burns and lacerations," the newscaster continued, "while the second was helivacked to Lucas County General, where he is in poor but stable condition. Although no evacuation of the park has been ordered, emergency officials fear an escalation of the fires in the next seventy-two hours."

At the unexpected news, Jo felt her heart sink like a stone. She was surprised at her reaction. A cold, nervous fear iced her blood, and it had nothing to do with the threat of fire. All of a sudden she wanted very much to know if Nick Kramer was all right.

What's up with you, Lofton? she berated herself angrily. Of course it's sad that a couple of guys got hurt. But you're getting much too worked up over a guy who's nothing special to you.

"I hope Nick's okay," Kayla said, rubbing it in.

Jo could see her adversary in the rubescent firelight, goading her with a knowing smile. Kayla was good at salting a wound.

Suddenly fed up, Jo stood and headed toward the cabin just to get a little time alone.

Hazel had to chuckle at the schoolyard silliness of it all. Watching these youngsters fight against and deny their feelings was more fun than anyone could buy a ticket for. Jo, with her natural shyness and that defensive, stiff-necked pride, was still smarting from

Ned Wilson's assault on her self-esteem, seeing Ned in every guy. And Nick, who appeared at a quick glance to be spoiled by good looks, but was in fact hungry with the same needs Jo felt.

This one's a challenge, Hazel conceded, fraught with touchy egos and hidden dangers. But she had never cared much for these "best friends" romances, where everything was sweet lavender and no storms. True love meant some fireworks and turbulence now and then, as surely as fast cars were made for speed, not safety.

"Time to take these gals out and dump them in the wild!" Hazel announced.

Jo was abandoned in a little, sloping pine hollow somewhere that she did not know from the moon.

All she had to do was get back to camp, she told herself. She was smart enough to be a teacher, so she was smart enough to use the map Mother Nature had given her. Hazel had taught her well, she thought, looking up at the dusting of stars in the sky.

This was easy enough to do. It was just that she had Nick Kramer on her mind, instead of what she was supposed to be doing. She couldn't stop worrying about that smoke jumper who was seriously hurt. Worrying that he had been Nick.

Shaking off her dread, she read the stars above her and said aloud as if to fortify herself, "This is the way."

She sighted on a big knoll well ahead, wending her

way through trees and bushes, the full moon making travel easy.

In fifteen minutes she reached the knoll.

Moving from point to point, she eventually reached a moonlit body of water: Wendigo Lake. It reflected in the moonlight like a liquid mirror. At her end she could see the narrow shadow of a dock. Beyond it, on the other side of the lake, was the paved road that wound up Lookout Mountain to Bridger's Summit. From there she could find her way with her eyes closed.

Jo felt exhilarated by the accomplishment. Something had been growing slowly within her these past days, something unfamiliar but welcome. She felt it very strongly now and realized, with a sense of wonder, that it was confidence.

She headed toward the long, wooden dock that jutted well out into the kidney-shaped lake.

Although she would never admit it to anyone, she wanted to get back to the campground and see if there was any word about Nick. More and more, she was starting to think it was he who had been injured earlier.

That grim possibility made her replay, in her mind, all the nasty comments she'd hurled at him.

There'd certainly been plenty, she admitted ruefully. And what, really, had he done to deserve them? Because Ned had put her through the wringer, she turned around and punished Nick.

Just ahead of her in the moonlit darkness, a figure stepped onto the dock.

He walked to the far end, near the water. Then abruptly he turned and looked her way.

"Humans or bears?" he called out in an amiable tone, for it was too dark to discern faces at a distance.

Jo drew up short at the sound of the voice from the dark end of the dock.

For a brief moment warm relief flooded her as she realized Nick was all right, after all.

But then, right on the heels of that emotion came a sudden, hot rush of anger as she realized she'd been set up.

Hazel had been the one to drop her off. She'd been the one to plan Jo's foray through the woods.

Jo would bet all the gold in Fort Knox that Hazel was playing matchmaker, and if Nick Kramer was playing along just to make her look like a fool, then he'd be sorry.

So very sorry, Jo thought as she stared at him in the moonlight, hands on her hips, waiting, silent accusation all over her face.

Ten

This was no chance encounter. Her guilt of seconds ago about mistreating Nick was swept away on a wave of indignation.

"Skinny-dipping, my brave firefighter?" she asked sarcastically.

"Well…I—" He held out his unused tackle.

"Yeah, right. You have some nerve," she fumed.

His silhouette was clear, backlit by silver moon-wash, slim-hipped and wide-shouldered. When he came toward her, moonlight limned his handsome profile, emphasizing the strong jaw, patrician nose, and his much-too-experienced lips.

Despite her anger and embarrassment, the memory of their torrid kiss on the bridge assailed her. Desire licked at her in a dizzying rush.

An awkward silence took over.

"Well, at least I know now you weren't hurt," she blurted out, not quite thinking.

"You thought maybe I was one of the ones who got it today? And you cared?" he said, astonished.

Is that a smile, she wondered, or just a little cynical pull of his lips? It was hard to tell, even though the moonlight was generous.

"Come here, girl," he said without demanding an answer to his question.

Even *she* knew her silence had answered well enough, anyway.

She dreaded being alone with him. He was a male she was infinitely attracted to, and she wasn't over Ned yet. It was coming at her way too fast.

For a few moments she felt herself balanced on a feather edge between excitement and apprehension. She was hurtling toward something, the same heady dizziness she'd initially felt during her affair with Ned.

One part of her liked it and wanted to keep hurtling; another part wanted to back out now and avoid the heartache that would surely come when she crashed.

"C'mon, walk with me around the lake," he said. "It's a fine night."

"I have to go to the other side, anyway, to get back to camp."

He laughed. "Does that mean yes?"

She shook her head, exasperated. Anything was

better than just staring at him in the moonlight. She was relieved to walk.

He speared his fingers through his hair, expelling a humorous sigh. "Ahh, I guess I should confess."

"Hazel set me up, didn't she."

"Oh, I s'pose she might have."

"Hazel's never fooled me," Jo asserted. "For a woman who never even considered dating after her husband was killed, she sure likes to play Cupid."

"And she's pretty damn good at it, if you ask me." He looked down at her, his face a hard, marble profile in the moonlight.

"I certainly feel snared," she answered, feeling wary.

A smile touched his lips. "Good."

Before she could say or do anything, he pulled her into his arms and hungrily sought her mouth with his.

The center of her being suddenly turned liquid, and her pulse exploded as if she'd been running hard.

For a few electrified moments she responded eagerly, probing his mouth with her tongue, pressing tightly against his muscular form, feeling herself mold to him, sharing his body heat.

Thrilling at the bulge of his arousal...

But then she seemed to be spinning out of control too quickly, and the apprehension was back.

This way misery lies, a voice cautioned.

It was the same, sudden pyrotechnics she'd felt with Ned, too, a hot need to tear off her clothes and make furious, intense, exhausting love for hours.

And just think how that all ended...

She pulled away from Nick and started walking again, fighting to get her breathing under control.

He simply fell in step beside her, matching her silence for some time, content with her company and the beautiful, moonlit lake, its calm surface reflecting diamond points of silver-white light.

There was a gentle, steady hum of insects, and now and then an owl hooted, the sound making a ghostly echo in the stillness. Occasionaly there was a plopping sound from the lake when a fish jumped.

He took her hand in his, and she let him, liking the strength and form of his grasp. The rough, callused spots reminded her how hard he worked with those hands.

"You know," he said after a minute or two, "I was thinking tonight how it must feel for you."

"What do you mean?"

"Well, for instance, like when all us guys ran into you on the bridge, all the ogling and smart remarks. They rib the hell out of me, too, but it's all basically harmless."

"Believe me," she said, "when it comes to the teasing, the guys aren't as bad as the women I'm camped with."

"Yeah, you mean...like Kayla catching us?"

"Yeah, like Kayla catching us," she repeated dryly. "I'll never hear the end of that."

It wasn't cold, but Jo shivered a little, and Nick must have sensed it, for he took off his denim jacket and draped it over her shoulders. Then he encircled her waist with his arm, drawing her closer as they strolled.

He brought her left arm around his own waist. He felt strong and supple, and everywhere she moved her hand, muscles rippled under it. Not bulked-up, weightlifting muscle, more like the compact strength of tempered steel.

"Hazel's a savvy old dame," he remarked, kissing her hair. "She's right, you know. We've been at each other's throats, and yet we don't even know each other."

"And, of course, being Hazel," Jo interjected, "she's at least hinted that I've had a relationship problem recently, right?"

"Something like that," he admitted. "But that happens to everybody. What really got me thinking was her mentioning it hasn't been much fun for you, growing up in Miss Montana's shadow."

"I love my mom, but thank God she wasn't Miss America, too, or I might be in a convent today."

They both laughed, easily and without forcing it, and it felt good to her. It felt good to have a strong pair of arms around her, too. Without knowing it, she'd been bottled up now for too long, emotionally and physically.

"So tell me about the guy," he said, nearly stopping her in her tracks.

She took a deep breath. Pulling her arm away from his waist, she said, "Blunt and unapologetic, spoken just like Hazel,'' she said. "No wonder she likes you."

"But he's the brick wall I have to get through, so it makes sense to cut to the chase."

She stopped and stared at him. "You're amazing. You just assume we're going to have some kind of affair, don't you? Well, let me tell you—"

He pulled her to him and kissed her.

In the insanity of the moment, she stopped protesting.

Finally, when they began walking once more, she released a frustrated moan and began her confession.

"Look, this guy isn't going to determine my life, okay? It wasn't a big deal. But there I was, totally gone on the guy, and he pulls out this wife and family like a rabbit out of a hat. But things like that happen all the time to women. This time it just happened to me."

"To be deceived that way," he said gently. "Must've really hurt."

She nodded. For a moment her mouth quivered, but not from the cold. The memory of Ned's sheepish, self-centered confession made old wounds throb anew. For some reason, with this man, she felt like talking about it. It was cathartic.

"It had happened at the beginning of the summer. I was taking my required continuing-ed courses at the state university. He was the charming, young visiting professor. I fell hard, and Ned pretended to have fallen, too. But in fact, the only thing I fell for was the oldest romantic con in the books. He was only in it for the sex. At the end of the summer term, when I wanted to talk about our future, he bluntly informed me he had a wife and kids back in Ohio."

She was quiet for a long time, the memories hurtling through her mind.

For some reason, some of them almost seemed funny to her now. "'But I'll be eternally grateful,'" she mimicked what Ned had told her with a straight face, "'for the kind way you validated my manhood. You'll always be so special to me.'" She almost laughed. "Can you believe it? He'd spoken to me as if he were signing the back of a publicity photo for a loyal fan."

Nick studied her.

After her confession she had a difficult time meeting his gaze.

"You must have been crushed," was all he said.

She closed her eyes, not revealing the half of it. Shy by nature, she'd been half tempted to become a hermit after the Ned disaster. Ned was weak and dishonest, but she couldn't help the persistent conviction that it was somehow all her fault. Her beauty-queen mother had imprinted upon her the notion that the only thing a man could devote himself to was eye candy—and eye candy was the last thing Jo cared to be.

"Well, I *won't* go through that again," she said, more for herself than for Nick. She looked at him. "And for all I know you've got a wife and twelve kids back in Mystery. So enough about me.'' She was eager to change the subject. ''I've been insulting you for days, but I'm supposed to know the enemy.''

He helped her over a fallen log, lifting her as effortlessly as a feather. She knew he was studying her in the ample moonlight, and her face, she hoped, mirrored nothing.

''Not a whole lot to know,'' Nick said quietly. ''When I was four years old, my parents were killed in a car accident up in the Canadian Rockies. It was one of those weekend getaways, you know, to celebrate their fifth anniversary. I was staying with my grandma Jane in Denver when it happened. I hate to admit it, but I have only the vaguest memories of them.''

His tone changed a little, hardened. ''So Grandma had custody of me until she had a stroke when I was fourteen. Child Protection Services had to take over then.''

''God, that must have been hard for you.''

''Tell me about it,'' he said. ''When you're a teenager, adoption is hardly likely. Most people want cute little babies, not a gangly adolescent with a chip on his shoulder. So I had a series of foster families, three in four years.''

He grew quiet as if the memories of that time were again fresh and raw.

Gently she offered, ''You must think me shallow, after what you've been through. Here I am,'' she muttered, "complaining about growing up in my mother's shadow."

"Hey, I don't remember them much, but Grandma told me my parents loved me, and I'm grateful I had them. And Grandma."

"What were your foster parents like?"

"Oh, I'm sure they meant well. I wasn't abused or anything like that. But to tell you the truth, I felt more like cheap labor than part of the family. My chief memories are of mowing lawns and washing cars and baby-sitting. Thank God I got a full scholarship for college when I turned eighteen. I've been on my own ever since."

"Kind of like a rolling stone that gathers no moss, right?" she probed.

"Something like that, maybe."

"So you don't have a wife and twelve kids somewhere?"

He laughed. "Frankly I'd probably really like that, but I'm afraid I don't have squat. When I get off this mountain, I have nothing waiting for me but a neglected cabin and an old mutt who spends more time in the kennel than with his master."

"I guess you aren't home much during the fire season. But do you ever think about settling down?"

"Are you kidding, lady? Does King Midas think about gold?"

"Yes, and so he hoards it. Why don't you go for your gold?"

"Maybe I'm not sure how to get it," he said. "I

did meet one woman I considered settling down for, maybe taking a teaching job, starting a family, all that. But I guess I stalled too long making up my mind, and she got sick and tired of dreading the evening news during fire seasons. Not to mention hardly seeing her boyfriend from spring until fall.'' His jaw hardened. ''Can't say I really blame her. No one else in my life has managed to stick around long.''

A silence wedged itself between them.

Nick suddenly seemed distant and cold, very much unlike the man who'd been pursuing her.

She wanted to say something to somehow bring him out of himself, but she stumbled on her words.

''My—my mother always called me a mouse. She never thought I was vivacious enough or popular enough—and the truth is, I wasn't. Not for her, anyway. But I realized one thing after Ned. It takes a lot of guts to be alone. My mother will never have the courage to do that.''

Nick stared at her for a long moment. Then, as if compelled, he raised his hand and ran his knuckles gently down her cheek.

He leaned to kiss her once more, and she felt the starry night swirling all around her like the whirlpools on the river. She sensed his hunger, and it deepened her own.

When she tried to pull away, he wouldn't let her go.

Her heart raced, and a giddy, nervous tightness filled her chest. She was pretty sure she knew what he planned on doing during his time with her tonight, and while she was against it in theory, with the moonlight and the soft bed of pine needles on her feet, theories were useless.

If she was truthful, a part of her longed for the warmth of physical contact and the ease of her loneliness, but another part of her sent up a red flag.

Now's your chance to back out, Jo lectured herself. You rushed things with Ned, too, and look how it turned out. You had to pick your heart up from his heels.

But all that was just sand in the wind. Nick's kiss still burned on her lips, and like a moth to a flame, she only wanted more of the fire.

"Why don't you forget about being courageous for the night?" Nick whispered.

She took his kiss, trembling with anticipation.

She said nothing more.

Eleven

Jo knew it was madness, craziness to lie with Nick on the soft carpet of pine needles, but she realized, as he pulled her down onto his spread-out jacket, that her need was an open invitation, an invitation that came from the core of her physical and emotional being.

He would not simply lie down with her and tease her like a kid in high school. Nick was a man and he would make love to her like a man, fully and deeply.

His intensity should have triggered more red flags, for she had surrendered once before to passion and lived to regret it. Instead of "once burned, twice shy," she seemed to be seeking the flame again like an addict, immersing herself in her destruction.

But Nick was different, she assured herself. Their talk tonight, just as Hazel had insisted, had shown how wrong both of them were about each other. It left Jo greatly relieved and yet feeling guilty for the insults and barbs. Her physical need seemed to converge with her emotional need to feel close to him, to make up for the wrong she'd done him.

"You cold?" he murmured as he kissed the sensitive skin on the side of her neck, tasting and smelling her, his breathing quickening when he pulled her closer.

"I think you're taking care of that," Jo teased.

She squirmed her hips invitingly and thrilled at the feel of his very noticeable arousal, opening her legs wider so he could press even closer against her.

"Yeah," he said, his voice husky, "and you just turned my thermostat way up."

"What's the matter, Hotshot, can't take the heat?"

"I'll be brave," he resolved, unbuttoning her shirt. "I have to warn you, I've been up in these mountains fighting fires a long time now. Once I get started, I may not want to quit. I hope you're feeling as greedy as I am."

She moaned as his hands slid inside her shirt. Before she knew it, he'd reached behind her and unfastened her bra. She felt her nipples stiffen instantly when he cupped her breasts and began rubbing his palms in little circles on the hardened nipples, sending electric shivers through her entire body.

She fumbled at unbuttoning his shirt, her hands

trembling with the pent-up hunger now being released.

She shuddered at the indescribable, intimate pleasure of pressing her naked flesh against his. Her hands traced the hard ridges of muscle cording his back, chest and shoulders. His stomach was flat and hard, and a mat of silky chest hair grew between rock-hard pecs.

He raised his face to kiss her mouth, and Jo looked up at him in the luminous moonlight, knowing she would never forget how handsome and desirable he looked in that moment. Like an exquisite bust combining the strength of Mars and the looks of Adonis.

And above him, the star-shot dome of a beautiful Montana night sky, with the pines soughing softly in the cool breeze. The chill against her bare skin was offset by the heat burning within her, and she knew that she could let this man take her naked in a snowdrift and she'd never notice the cold until it was too late.

This time they kissed for countless minutes, tongues probing greedily as they pressed more and more urgently together, as if he was already inside her.

Jo fumbled his belt loose while he, in turn, unbuttoned her jeans and tugged them over her hips.

"At this point," he said reluctantly, "isn't one of us supposed to bring up birth control?"

"Surely," she teased, "the babe slayer has several condoms in his wallet?"

Guilt stabbed her briefly when she realized she sounded like Kayla.

"See, I only bring a dozen with me on each job," he teased right back, "and I'm fresh out. Guess I need to order by the gross."

"Not to worry," she assured him. "I'm on the pill."

She hardly felt like explaining right then that she was only on the pill since meeting Ned, or that she meant to stop taking them once her current prescription ran out. All that would have to wait.

In fact, she was incapable of even thinking clearly as his hand glided under the elastic waistband of her panties and down to the damp center of her need.

She opened her legs wider, gasping with pleasure when his fingers teased her soft folds open like petals to the sun. He lowered his mouth over one of her nipples, sucking and teasing it as his fingers moved more and more urgently between her legs, making her hard nubbin swell.

"Nick...Nick." She whispered his name over and over like a chant.

An intense climax suddenly crashed down on her, the pleasure bending her almost double and immediately making her hungry for more, even as she gasped for breath.

He slid his briefs down and placed her hand on his rock hard length to feel his need throbbing. He was powerful in her hand, saber-curved, excitingly hard.

She was so anxious for him it chilled her. She

opened her legs wide in the night air, and a moment later all she knew was incomparable pleasure as he slid into her, no teasing, but going in deeply the way she wanted, filling her with nothing but man.

He moved against her, his breath hard and fast, as if he was holding himself back. His hard body rubbed along her soft chest, creating a frisson of eroticism that had nothing to do with her loins.

Taking her mouth in a last heated kiss, his pumping became increasingly faster and furious. She jockeyed along to wherever he went, her own pleasure coming in waves that seemed to never end.

Unable to take it much more, she cried out at the pleasure, moving her hands to his hard-flexing gluteus muscles, and encouraging him to keep driving deep and hard.

She had no idea how many times she climaxed before he spent himself in several final, hard plunges, crying out her name and then spasming violently in the powerful aftermath of his orgasm, as if his body circuits were overloaded.

She herself had never climaxed so quickly and repeatedly with any man, and yet, feeling greedy as he'd wanted her to, she secretly wished he would not stop even after his release.

He seemed to understand her muscles holding him in, silently asking him not to slide out of her, and suddenly her need excited him to full arousal again. Almost without any pause, he began the pleasure rhythm again, hard and ready.

She lost all track of time after that, rising again and again to peaks of almost unbearable pleasure, then almost blacking out in a daze before one of them would start all over again.

It was literally pure, mindless pleasure. The two of them were one, and nothing else existed.

But at the back of her mind, like the tag end of some pop tune, she kept hearing a warning voice. All she could understand, however, was its urgent tone, for the words themselves were lost in the pounding of her heart.

"I don't believe it."

Nick's voice sounded thick with sleep, almost drugged.

"It's 3 a.m.," he told her, kissing her eyelids open. "We've been here almost six hours."

Six hours, Jo thought with little reaction at first. A moment later, however, she sat up, buttoning her shirt and shivering in the damp chill.

"Six hours," she repeated, suddenly feeling like a teenager who had missed curfew. "I guess we...lost track of time."

They both laughed self-consciously at her silly understatement, and he kissed her. Instantly, despite the mild ache between her legs, she wanted him again. But the thought of what possibly waited up at the cabins cooled her ardor.

Shivering even more as nervousness was added to

the cold, she took his extended hand and rose to her feet, quickly straightening and buttoning her clothing.

He must have read her thoughts, judging from his next remark. "They're probably all asleep, you know. Which doesn't mean you won't get razzed tomorrow. I know I will. The guys in my crew don't miss a thing."

"You're right," Jo decided, feeling brave. "I'm sure Hazel would tell them I was with you, anyway, so I'll just sneak quietly into bed and face the music tomorrow."

They set off hand in hand, following the switch-backing blacktop road that wound its way up to Bridger's Summit.

"You sorry?" he asked.

"Abject with remorse," she deadpanned, and they both laughed again, stopping to kiss.

In truth she felt that her feet weren't even touching the ground. She'd made love with him for hours and the world went away. The hurting went away. She wanted to do it again and again until…

She noticed he'd turned quiet. Gently he led her along the road to the cabin.

His silence began to rattle her.

All sorts of demons appeared in her mind. The worst demon of all was the fear of tomorrow. Of never seeing him again, of realizing she'd just been had for a one-night stand.

She watched him, their breaths forming faint wraiths in the waning moonlight.

They were near the summit now, and she could make out the faint outlines of the two cabins through the cluster of pines ahead. Beyond them she could see the faint glimmer in the east known as false dawn.

"I think we best say good-night out here in the road," Jo suggested. "I don't want to get caught with you. I'll have to fess up soon enough, but I'll need some sleep first."

The first pang of remorse tightened her heart. Staring at him, she felt cold reality seep in. The question circled silently overhead like a vulture.

When am I going to see you again?

She'd behaved impetuously, and imprudent acts were usually paid for in a pound of flesh. She hardly knew him. They'd fallen together in the moonlight, in the heat of loneliness.

Right now she wondered if what they'd shared had even been real, let alone if it was something with substance, something that would last.

Is this going to be it? she wondered, a chill overtaking her.

Or would they just keep meeting when they could, maybe have a wild little fling in the boonies until it was time for her to go back to Mystery?

Would the whole experience be chalked up to good times, and they'd never see each other again?

Perhaps she was ready to revise her opinion about men. Maybe it was enough to have just the best sex in the world and nothing else. After Ned, maybe that was all she needed. No heart involved. Just freewheeling physical pleasure, no strings. That might be best. Low emotional expectations but high-power orgasms, to avoid the heartache.

Acting far more bravely than she felt, she finally summoned the courage to speak the dreaded question. "So when I am going to—"

"Look," he said, cutting her off, "I have to tell you my schedule up here is pretty mercurial. I can't plan any kind of date until the fires are all out. But I'd still like to see you if I can."

Pain shot through her heart like a thunderbolt. She knew what he was saying. If she was convenient, he'd come around again. But there were no plans. There was really nothing between them but sex.

So maybe she should be relieved, instead of hurt, she scolded herself. It was easier this way. More direct, less messy. Minimum involvement, maximum fun.

"We'll see how it goes, then," she said evenly, not showing a trace of her wounded feelings.

He paused as if he had something on his mind that he was burning to let out. Finally he said, "I know Hazel keeps you busy, but there's a good café in Stony Rapids. We've got a van I can use, parked at the ranger station. How 'bout lunch tomorrow? I don't go on duty until six down in the canyon."

"I don't know," she murmured, not sure if she could keep the act up. "Maybe that would work. We've got a break tomorrow because Hazel and her cronies are going into town to buy…uh, Neat's-foot oil and a few other weird things like that.''

''Neat's-foot oil isn't weird, townie. You use it to waterproof leather. I rub it on my boots all the time.''

''I know,'' Jo said, nervousness tickling her stomach as she thought about the Chute. ''We'll be waterproofing ours, too, for the river rafting.''

''Piece of cake,'' he assured her. Then he smiled. ''So maybe I'll see you tomorrow?''

''Looks like it, Mr. Fireman.'' She studied him, wondering if his plans for lunch involved a stop at the hourly motel. The tawdriness of it crippled her heart even more. She wasn't sure she could go through with it.

Minimum involvement, maximum fun needed a stone-cold heart. And so far, from the hurt she felt inside, hers still had a bit of warmth in it.

''Between ten and ten-thirty, okay?''

''Sure. Sweet dreams.'' She made to walk away, but he grabbed her hand and pulled her to him. He kissed her. She wanted the willpower to cut it short, but instead, her need grew for more. He seemed to trigger her like some wild animal in heat.

''See you at ten.'' He finally pulled away and retreated down the road.

She turned toward the cabins and again felt the knife through her heart. There was no denying her passion for him, but she was vulnerable, especially now. She was bound to make the wrong choices, and going to town with him for a quickie didn't seem like the right choice.

But when he showed up at ten, she would go with him, she knew it. He would kiss her, and she would want him. And for an hour, he would make the hurt go away, until it fired anew with a vengeance.

Nonetheless, she couldn't help feeling the irony of the situation. Hazel had lectured Kayla and the others on the "true purpose" of this trip into the wilderness; now her main protégée was slinking home in the dark, guilty as sin, man scent still clinging to her.

They're all asleep, she assured herself as she approached her cabin.

But somehow she knew explaining herself wouldn't be that easy. Because even she didn't understand what she had done.

Twelve

Jo, shivery with cold and nervousness, seemed to step on every loud, snapping stick on the way to the cabin. Although the girls had been told they would be allowed to sleep a little later than usual in the morning, there were still only a few hours' rest remaining. She knew she'd pay for her tryst with tiredness and achy muscles, but right now she was wide awake.

Recurring memories and images made her pulse race.

She knew she desired more erotic pleasure with him. Just thinking about how he felt, his hard length moving inside her, made her want to turn around and go sneak into his sleeping bag.

But his catch-you-when-I-can attitude was heart-rending. Indeed, he did shoulder heavy responsibilities as a firefighter. She knew their relationship would have to take a back seat to disaster. But the forest fires couldn't last forever. At some point the noncommittal attitude would either deepen into commitment and a real relationship, or she would know she was just another notch on the bedpost and not get her hopes up.

Deep inside, she wasn't sure she could endure being another notch. She wanted to be more important to Nick than just a fading memory of a lusty night under the stars. Yet at the moment, she had only two choices. She either had to cut and run now or risk falling more deeply into the quagmire of lust and love.

Unfortunately, as she faced the closed door of her cabin, her instincts raged for salvation. As she'd learned from Ned, she couldn't predict him or his feelings, and she could only control her own. Certainly it would be far easier to control them—and halt them—now if she never saw him again.

Unable to decide, she pushed open the door. It was silly, yet she couldn't help feeling self-conscious. There could be no question whatsoever, if anyone saw her now, about where she'd been, or with whom, or what they'd been up to. She might as well have a sign taped to her: I'VE BEEN DOING IT.

The door sounded like the meow of a cat as she nudged it closed, rusted hinges protesting. Moonlight flooded the interior through both uncurtained windows, a pale, ghostly blue. It all seemed so peaceful and proper, pristine even, that she felt more guilt poke at her.

She heard the even, steady breathing of her sleeping companions. Softly as she could, Jo crept across the bare wooden floor, wincing each time a board creaked.

Why did everything sound so damn loud at night? Even her thoughts seemed to make noise in the quiet cabin.

So far so good. Quickly she undressed and slid beneath the covers, fluffing up her pillow.

"Better brush the twigs out of your hair, nature girl."

Jo practically cried out in fright at the unexpected words, spoken just above a whisper. To her primed ears, they were as loud as screams.

Kayla.

Of course. The girl had probably lain awake all these hours, just to make her wisecracks.

Jo felt her cheeks heat, but she tried to ignore the taunting remark.

Then Kayla spoke out loud.

"I guess you learned all about the stars, being on your back all night long. Tell me, did the earth move?"

"Please, just leave me—"

"It's been obvious from day one that you intended

to do the deed with that man. All your sneaking around hasn't fooled anybody."

"Hey!" Bonnie's sleepy voice protested. "Shut up, Kayla, people are trying to sleep."

"Me? What about *her* sneaking in here in the middle of the night?"

Bonnie, wide awake now and no fan of Kayla's, anyway, sat up in bed.

"Pipe down! Honest to God, Kayla, you're worse than a little kid. Ain't no virgins at this party, right? So let's just all go to sleep."

Kayla fumed. "I'll have you know—"

"Hey! I gotta conk some heads together or what? Us old dames need our beauty rest."

Hazel's authoritative voice sounded from the doorway, silencing all of them. To Jo, she sounded more amused than angry. She could see the vague outline of Hazel's form and her long, white pullover sleep shirt.

"Bury the hatchet, ladies," Hazel said cheerfully from the door. "And not in each other. But if you must, please do it during daylight hours."

She said good-night and returned to her cabin.

Jo waited, filled with dread, for Kayla to start all over again. But apparently hostilities had ceased for now. At least, she consoled herself, the fact of her little dalliance tonight was now announced, sparing her the revelation later. On the other hand, it was also now guaranteed to be remembered by one and all.

Exhaustion quickly claimed her, and she drifted off

to sleep with the anticipation of nightmares. Nick was now foremost in her thoughts, and her last unfinished thought was that tomorrow she'd decide if they'd ever be together again.

Exhausted, Nick fell into a deep, dreamless sleep almost as soon as he rolled into his down-stuffed sleeping bag. In what seemed no time at all, someone was calling out his name and shaking him awake.

"Nick! Hey, wake up, Romeo! We got trouble."

"Huh? Wha—?"

Nick struggled to sit up. Tom Albers and Jason Baumgarter stood just outside the fly of his tent. The sun was up, but only barely. It gave feeble light and no warmth.

"Mike Silewski's on the horn," Jason said, holding out the field radio handset. "Wants to talk at you."

For a few moments, still feeling drugged with deep sleep, Nick had to search his memory. Then he recalled Silewski was the senior park ranger in the Bitterroot.

"Yeah, Mike?" he managed. But he had to repeat himself, for in his sluggish state he forgot to depress the talk switch.

"Man, you sound rough. Tough night?"

Nick could hear the grin in the ranger's tone, but it wasn't very amusing to him at the moment. How did these guys always know things so fast?

"If you get near a point," Nick reminded him impatiently, "feel free to make it."

"Touchy, touchy. We've got a pocket burn about two klicks north of the summit," Silewski reported. "Airborne embers, evidently, kicked up by that wind last night. Mostly it's just old-growth timber on that mountain, and we could let it thin itself out. But Fort Liberty's smack in the middle of the pocket."

"Yeah, I know the place."

Nick came fully awake at the grim news. Historic Fort Liberty had been built just after the Civil War as a far-north outpost for the U.S. Sixth Cavalry. The jewel of Montana pride and tourism, it was also one of the finest nineteenth-century restorations in the American West. As such, it attracted tourists and, from time to time, Hollywood filmmakers, and brought badly needed revenue into Montana.

"We've got a priority request from the governor to protect that site," Silewski added. "Your team will insert by helicopter, since there's no safe drop zone. Your orders are to build a firebreak around the fort and then dig in until the danger's past. You guys should be ready to stage in thirty minutes."

Nick had been a smoke jumper too long to question orders. But he immediately felt a sharp stab of disappointment. There went his time today with Jo. And an opportunity he had been thinking about for several days, the chance to know her better.

"I know you guys're s'posed to be off until later," Silewski said. "But the governor is worried sick, and we can't pull Winkler's team off mop-up—they're still finding hot spots.''

''You know our motto,'' Nick replied stoically. ''Always flexible. Look, Mike, do me a little favor?''

''At your service, Hotshot.''

''I'm going to leave a note in an envelope at our campsite. I'll tape it to that tree that's been split by lightning. Would you take it up to one of the women who's camped on Bridger's Summit?''

''Aha! This hot Texan blonde I'm hearing about, right?''

''No, another one. Her name'll be on the envelope. Deliver it to her personally.''

''Tough assignment,'' Silewski said drolly, ''but I guess I'm man enough to do it.''

''Stout lad,'' Nick replied. ''Over and out.''

While Tom and Jason woke up the rest of the team, Nick dug out his letter-writing supplies and penned a quick note to Jo, explaining about the emergency. He assured her he'd be back before she was due to return to Mystery and told her how disappointed he was at the interruption of their time together.

''I hope, more than anything,'' he wrote in closing, ''that what we had together last night was just the beginning of our relationship, not the end. The fire season won't last that much longer, and I hope you'll want me to come see you in Mystery. I really want a place in your life if you want me in it.''

He folded the note, sealed it in an envelope and

wrote Jo's name on the envelope. Still bitterly disappointed, and resenting this assignment right now in his life, he started assembling his gear.

Mike Silewski parked the U.S. Park Service Blazer in the lot beside the cabins atop Lookout Mountain. With Nick's note tucked into his shirt pocket, he climbed out of the vehicle and removed his sunglasses for a better look at the pleasant sight coming toward him across the camp clearing.

The woman carried a water jar, evidently headed for the pump down the slope. It had to be the same busty blonde all the guys were talking about.

Trim legs tanned a golden brown poured out of denim short-shorts so tight they left little to the imagination. And her short-sleeve white blouse was rolled up and tied to reveal a smooth, flat midriff.

"Can I do something for you, Ranger?" she asked with a sexy smile and ambiguous phrasing, and Mike had to swallow a couple of times before he could find his voice and answer.

"Uh, hi, there."

The ranger glanced behind her. He saw another woman, young like this one, playing tetherball with a ball and rope tied to a tree.

"I've got a note here from Nick Kramer," he explained. "I take it you aren't Jo Lofton?"

For just a fraction of a second, her charming smile seemed to waver. But it was back so quickly Silewski thought maybe she'd just squinted at the morning sun-light.

"No, I'm Kayla," the blonde introduced herself. "Jo's not here right now, but I'll be glad to give her the note when she returns to camp."

Her dazzling white teeth flashed as she poured him an even wider smile.

"I'm sure that would be just fine," he replied. "Thanks a lot."

He handed her the letter, trying not to be too blatant about ogling her body. Not that she seemed at all offended by his interest. Quite the contrary, her atti-tude seemed to be: enjoy it, that's what it's for.

"I'll see she gets it," Kayla promised again as the ranger got back into his vehicle.

But as he backed out of the lot, Kayla tossed a glance back over her shoulder to see if any of the others had seen him give her something.

Bonnie still playing tetherball, was not even aware she was still there. And Kayla had deliberately lied— Jo was still inside the cabin, moping about something. No doubt this letter from Nick had something to do with it.

Kayla quickly headed down the path toward the stone bridge, wanting to put trees between herself and the rest. She glanced at the envelope in her hand, and a mixture of anger, jealousy and guilt lanced through her. The anger and the jealousy far outweighed the guilt.

Anger made Kayla frown as she recalled last night in the cabin, how all of them had ganged up against her. Even Hazel. Jo comes slinking in just before dawn, yet they all turned on her, Kayla.

"Who in hell do they think they are?" she fumed out loud as she made up her mind.

She glanced back one more time to make sure no one was around. Then she set the water jar down and tore the envelope open.

Thirteen

Jo had expected to sleep in, especially since Hazel and her cronies were giving them a rare break from the usual shock reveille. But the commotion of the other girls getting up and dressed, not that long after sunrise, brought her awake, too. Rather than just lying there pretending to sleep, she decided to tough it out and get up with the others.

She got a reprieve from Kayla's taunts, however, for unbelievably, she was already up and gone. She'd even neatly made her bed before she left.

"Yeah, I know," Bonnie greeted her, reading the surprise in Jo's face. "Our little Texas Twinkie has evidently turned over a new leaf. I didn't even hear her leave."

But Kayla's blessed absence could not buoy Jo's already crushed feelings. Somehow, in the cold light of morning, she realized she had to stay sane. When Nick showed up for her at ten, she'd decided to tell him to call her when he got off the mountain and could pursue a real relationship. She couldn't see him until then. She just wasn't that hard yet.

Ned had never once suggested seeing her anywhere but in his apartment on campus. At the time she simply assumed it was because he didn't want to announce he was dating one of his students.

But in fact, he'd had no need of her that couldn't be met in the bedroom. She would have seen that if she hadn't made the stupid mistake of assuming he felt what she felt.

She was not going to make that mistake with Nick.

"I might as well confess now and get it over with," she announced to her friends just before she left for the showers. "Nick's dropping by later."

"Hey, thanks, chum," Bonnie protested with mock annoyance. "So what about, oh, lonesome me? You could at least fix me up with that cute radio guy, Jason. He's got dimples when he smiles."

Jo laughed as she left the cabin.

A surprise awaited her when she crossed the camp clearing: Kayla had built up the fire left by the older women from breakfast and was scrambling eggs in a big iron skillet.

"Breakfast'll be ready in a jiff," she said to Jo, not glancing in her direction but speaking in a civil tone. It would have surprised Jo at any time, but especially now, after the altercation earlier this morning. Now there was not one sign that Kayla was annoyed at her.

"Thanks," Jo replied in a carefully neutral tone.

She showered, washed and conditioned her hair, then donned the only dress she had brought along, a blue slip dress. It felt good to put on her sandals, instead of hiking boots. She even spritzed her hair back.

Determined to feel as good as she could about the direction she was going in, she even dabbed on a little coral lipstick. Obviously she might never see Nick after she told him he could call her and that was all he was going to get. But at least their parting wouldn't be like Ned and hers, with her crushed and weeping. No, she was going to look great, smile and control everything inside until she was alone. And if he never called her, only then would she let out the hurt.

After she emerged from the shower hut, Jo joined the others for breakfast but only had a cup of coffee. It was already nearly ten, and she expected Nick any minute.

She also still expected a confrontation of some kind with Kayla, but it never happened. Although not exactly friendly, for she still avoided looking at Jo, Kayla didn't aim any of the usual smug glances in her direction.

If this was an olive branch, Jo was happy to accept

it. But somehow it didn't add up right. It didn't make sense that, suddenly this morning, Kayla would be in the mood for peace.

As Hazel had pointed out, Kayla did have her sweet points. Maybe, Jo decided, I should stop judging her so harshly.

Breakfast ended, and Bonnie went out to collect firewood. As if uncomfortable being alone with Jo, Kayla went back into the cabin, leaving Jo alone with the morning peace and stillness.

At first she enjoyed the solitude. But more time ticked by, and as it did her state of mind gradually changed from determined expectation to resentment.

It hadn't occurred to her that Nick wouldn't show. For some stupid reason she thought she'd be the one to direct the relationship, if they even had a relationship. She'd never expected to be dumped right after her one-night stand.

But maybe she should have, she thought. Naive, that was her, through and through. Ned wouldn't have gotten so far with her if she hadn't mistaken him for an honorable man.

Now, with every minute that passed, it seemed she'd mistaken Nick for an honorable man, too.

By eleven o'clock, her hurt increased tenfold. By eleven-forty-five, anger warred with all that hurt.

By this point she felt stupid hanging around outside, drawing attention to the fact that Nick had stood her up. Trying to keep her feelings out of her face, she joined the others in the cabin. She dug a paperback out of her pack and stretched out on her bed, pretending to read.

"Hazel and the others will be back before too long," Bonnie said hesitantly, looking up from her crossword-puzzle book. "Maybe you should walk down to Nick's camp?"

"Oh, he probably just overslept." Jo managed to make it sound like no big deal. "I might just as well stay here. I'm sure he'll turn up later. We'll talk then, I suppppose."

"Talk?" Bonnie looked at her. Her eyes asked questions.

Why, Jo chastised herself, did she have to tell them Nick was coming at ten? Now there was this gathering sympathy for her, even though she was devastated enough right now without having to endure pity to boot.

At least Kayla's curiosity remained muted. She definitely was not rubbing it in—just keeping completely to herself and listening to her CD player through headphones while painting her nails. She did not even glance at Jo.

Jo stared at the same page for countless minutes, not seeing a word. At one point heat suddenly formed behind her eyes and her vision blurred as tears threatened. Only with a supreme effort of will did she maintain her composure.

Don't lose it, she commanded herself harshly.

She could not understand how this could be. All Nick's attention and intensity only last night, and now all of it was simply gone like a fist when you open your hand.

The silence in the cabin became unbearable, and Bonnie decided to dispel it.

"You getting nervous about the Chute, Jo?" she inquired. "I sure am. It's the day after tomorrow."

"Yeah, I'm sweating it," Jo replied, though she hadn't even spared a thought for it lately. The heady waters of romance had been challenge enough.

"Swoop-for-your-life…not a very confidence-inspiring name," Sheryl chimed in.

"Nick said…"

Jo hesitated, surprising herself, for the words had come out almost on their own. But she did not dare leave the sentence hanging. That would be even worse.

"Nick said the same thing Hazel does." She forced her tone to sound casual. "He calls the Stony Rapids an easy river for rafting."

Bonnie, bless her, did an excellent job of pretending she'd noticed nothing.

"Huh! That's easy for him to say—a guy who jumps out of planes and risks death for a living. And Hazel, well, she's sweet and I love her, but she's a McCallum. My God, those ranchers are hard as woodpeckers' lips. Me, I'm just a timid hairstylist."

"You've done fine so far," Jo assured her, wanting to steer away from the topic of Nick. "We're gonna have fun rafting the Chute, you'll see."

It amazed her, the disconnect between her calm remarks and her turmoiled interior. And such hypocrisy—she no more cared about making that rafting trip than she cared to memorize a phone book.

Right now she wanted only one thing. One person. Nick. She wanted him to suddenly show up and explain away all of this letdown. And when she finally heard the crunch of gravel under tires out in the parking area, her heart leaped into her throat.

Until she recognized Hazel and Dottie's voices and realized it was just the older gals returning from town.

Hazel and Dottie had just exited the supermarket in town when a U.S. Forest Service bus rolled past, filled with smoke jumpers wearing their familiar orange-and-blue T-shirts. It was headed east, out of town, not west toward the high-timber country where the fires raged. And the guys were dressed to travel, not to fight fires.

When Hazel was back at the camp, she decided a little patrol was in order. Dottie didn't have to ask where she was going.

Hazel followed the hiking trail down the slope from Bridger's Summit, a series of switchbacks through pine and aspen. The smoke jumpers' camp was only about five minutes from the mountaintop cabins.

Or *had* been.

The matriarch emerged from behind a huge dead-fall of brush and brambles, then stood staring at the clearing, her disappointment sudden and keen.

The spot was deserted. Only a few flattened spots in the grass even hinted that tents had been pitched here.

So maybe Nick had indeed pulled stakes and left for good. Taken the "geographical cure," as her cowboys called it when a man left town suddenly after feeding a line of bull to a woman he'd seduced.

And yet…she was reluctant to form that conclusion just yet. Nick had seemed so sincere and decent when she talked to him.

But was it all just moonshine?

I was so worried about Jo retreating under a shell, she told herself. Maybe, though, I stupidly forgot *why* she needed that shell in the first place. And just maybe I coaxed her out only to get crushed again.

"Looks like he cut and ran, huh?"

Jo's voice, just behind her, startled Hazel back to the present moment. She turned to confront her younger friend, saw the dejected look on Jo's face.

"Now, honey, don't go stacking your conclusions higher than your evidence."

"Oh, Hazel, he had you fooled even before he deceived me. Face it, we've both been bamboozled by a master jerk."

"Before you hang the no-good label on him, shouldn't you wait a bit?"

Jo tried to form a cynical smile, but abandoned the effort. "You know the old joke. 'Denial' is not a river in Egypt."

"Jo, honey, if all Nick wanted was to get laid, why did he spurn a hot-to-trot sure thing like Kayla and direct all his efforts to you?"

"Challenge, Hazel. The thrill of the hunt. He was telling me the truth when he said he didn't like sure things. I'll give him that much credit—he doesn't do the easy and obvious thing.''

Despite Jo's bitter tone, Hazel knew her angry response might well contain a nugget of truth. Looking at the young teacher now, as she gazed at the deserted clearing, came close to breaking Hazel's heart.

''What really hurts,'' Jo confided in a rush of brokenhearted candor, ''is the way I so foolishly thought the two of us had made an emotional connection. Isn't that hilarious? That's why the sex was so special, for me, anyway. The same stupid, *stupid* mistake I made with Ned and vowed never to repeat.''

''Jo, you shouldn't—''

''But I, Jo Lofton, small-town music teacher and old maid in training, am not Miss Montana material,'' Jo rushed on, her tone bitter as she mocked herself. ''Little simps like me are only good for a quick poke before the stud muffins move on to the next love-struck sucker or go back home to the little woman.''

Hazel put an arm around Jo's shoulders and squeezed. Although she had not yet leaped to the same conclusions Jo obviously had, it certainly looked as if Jo's bitterness might be justified.

Maybe the pessimistic historians were right, Hazel thought glumly. Maybe human beings *don't* learn from history. And individuals, like civilizations, were doomed by their own personalities, forced to repeat the same disastrous mistakes over and over.

Jo's next comment seemed to confirm Hazel's thought.

''It's not that I don't know the reality,'' she lamented, close to tears. "I just keep denying it. Why?"

"Because you're a wonderful girl with high ideals about love," Hazel responded firmly. "And because your basic nature is to trust others. That's not unusual in trustworthy individuals like yourself. Personally, I hope you never change."

"Oh, God, Hazel, I'd *better* change. I can't take any more of—of—"

But Jo couldn't finish her thought before a sob tore from her throat, unleashing a torrent of tears. Feeling as if a knife was twisting inside her, for her own guilt was so strong, Hazel held the miserable girl in a mother's hug, trying to comfort her.

I caused this, Hazel realized, not Nick. My crusade to save Mystery, to populate it with married couples of my secret choosing—I put that ambition over Jo's emotional well-being. Even if Nick did cut and run, as the mounting evidence suggested, Hazel felt it was her job to see it coming. But she had failed.

In her pride and scheming, she had failed Jo. And pride, Hazel reminded herself, comes directly from the devil. And like a good devil, I've helped send this innocent girl to the hell of a broken heart, exposed her to the bitter test of betrayal.

"C'mon, hon," Hazel said gently, turning Jo back toward the summit. "I think both of us need to stay busy for a while."

Fourteen

As soon as Nick's team was inserted by helicopter into the thick timber surrounding Fort Liberty, they got down to the hard, backbreaking work of creating a firebreak—a swath of cleared ground completely encircling the fort.

This involved first clearing the thick brambles and other fuel, for the larger trees would not easily ignite without natural kindling. It was intense, blistering labor that had to be done quickly because flames were closing in fast.

So Nick split his group into two teams of six, one hour on, one hour off, one well-rested group always at work. He had learned from experience that six rested men could outwork twelve tired ones.

Despite the intense effort, however, his mind was occupied with constant thoughts of Jo Lofton.

Just my luck, he thought more than once. Finally he'd met someone who was the kind he'd like to settle down with, and this damned assignment had to pop up. He felt like a kid with a neat new toy, but those damned grown-ups weren't letting him play with it.

At least, he consoled himself, he was able to get an explanatory note to her. Even so, he felt he'd let Jo down by missing their date. He'd let himself down, too. He wanted to know more about her. It was hard to wait.

Damn this job, anyway. It had driven a wedge between him and Karen, too.

"This is a fine job if you're a woman-hater," he remarked sarcastically during one of his team's rest periods.

"Hey, you want some cheese to go with that whine?" Jason teased him. "Your little sugarplum will taste just as sweet when we get back to Lookout Mountain."

Nick, Jason and four others sat eating their bland military rations in a small base camp they had quickly established. They were grimy, their hair sweat-plastered.

"Yeah, if she's still there," Nick groused. "We could be up here for days if that wind shifts."

They had been ordered by the fire-command center on Copper Mountain to hold their position until relieved. Nick had no idea when that would be. Flames were unpredictable.

"Even if she's gone," Jason reminded him, "you know where she lives, right?"

"Yeah," Nick conceded, finding some comfort in the reminder. "I've never been to the town of Mystery, but Jo says it's small. It won't be hard to locate her. How many music teachers can they have?"

"Question is, how many have *you* had?" a smoke jumper named Brian Aldritch said, and the others snickered.

"One was enough," Nick shot back.

All the guys hooted at that one, but Nick wasn't in the mood for the usual macho razzing. No, he thought, finding Jo would not be the real problem. What truly worried him was trying to find out what was in his own heart. Again he realized he had been searching for one good reason to give up his transient lifestyle and sink down roots someplace.

Face it, he lectured himself, you're not going to find what you've never had unless you stop running.

And he didn't want to run with Jo. She was the first woman he'd felt this way about. Sure, he thought he'd wanted to settle down with Karen, but all the missed dates, all the staying on the mountain to work extra shifts, that had been running from her, too. He'd liked the idea of settling down, but he now knew Karen hadn't been the one. And that was why she got fed up.

But Jo was different. She was the "one good reason'' he'd been searching for all his life. But could he measure up to his dream? Security, trust, commitment—these were not things included in his background. When Karen had forced him into a choice— either her or his job—it was his fear that made him choose the latter.

With Jo, however, the feelings were strong enough to face that fear. But did she reciprocate his feelings? Sure, the sex had been intense. However, it was still too soon to know if she wanted what he wanted. He was no expert on the female psyche, but he had learned one hard fact from Karen: the woman usually held the ''power''. It was she who decided if a relationship had a chance.

''Baker One Actual, this is Baker One,'' came a static-fuzzy, familiar voice over Jason's radio transceiver. Mike Silewski...

Nick took the handheld unit from Jason and pressed the talk switch.

''Baker One, this is Baker One Actual,'' Nick responded. ''Read you loud and clear, Mike.''

''Howzit goin' up there, stout lads? Governor Collins is calling us every hour for a report. He's worried sick.''

''Tell him to calm down, the pros from Dover have the situation well in hand. Hey, did you deliver that note?''

''Relax, studly, I delivered it. Say, you boys are missing all the fun. Bridger's Summit is crawling with hot little numbers. Man, that Texas blonde gave me a look I could feel in my hip pocket. Think I'll head back up there while you schmucks are busting your humps.''

Jason swore and grabbed the radio.

''Hey, Mike? You can't see this, but we're all flipping you the bird, pal.''

''Right back atcha, Hotshots. Over and out.''

''Time to hit it, boys,'' Nick said, consulting his watch. He stretched the stiffness from his back, then shouldered his modified ax, one side cutting blade, the other a pick.

The last thing a fireslayer needed was a woman on his mind, but Nick knew he was going into the mouth of hell with one terrible Achilles' heel. Jo would not be banished from his thoughts.

Nor, he hoped, from his life.

After verifying that Nick and his team had apparently struck their camp and departed, Jo and Hazel returned together to their own camp.

''We'll get out on the river, keep you busy,'' Hazel consoled her. ''I know it won't be much fun, sweet love, but it'll be better than moping around thinking about things.''

The rest of the afternoon was reserved for practicing emergency rescues before the younger women braved the Chute day after tomorrow, the most turbulent stretch of the river during the almost three-hour rafting trip to the floor of Crying Horse Canyon.

Jo really did try to get into the spirit. But all of it

seemed unreal, somehow, as if she was just an actress pretending to have fun.

Bonnie leaned over and said low in her ear, ''She must be over her PMS!''

Bonnie shifted her eyes enough to remind Jo how close the thwart behind them, where Kayla sat, was. Even Jo, distracted though she was, had noticed what Bonnie was alluding to. Everyone had by now. Kayla, usually overflowing with gripes, complaints and criticism, seemed to have withdrawn into herself. And shock of all shocks, she was being cooperative and civil.

Now Jo shrugged and said, ''Who knows? She's stopped riding me, so I hope whatever it is keeps up.''

But Bonnie's allusion to PMS made Jo suddenly nervous. She was still on the pill, yes, but had she taken them all lately? Since the end of her affair with Ned, she had been careless at times because she was only using up the last of her supply.

The question hadn't nagged her when she and Nick were close; now, with him evidently riding off into the sunset like a cowboy at the end of a Western, fear clutched at her.

Please, she prayed fervently, don't let me be pregnant—especially not now.

Hazel and the others were conferring quietly in their raft nearby, Hazel pointing off to the north. Jo glanced in that direction and saw a thick, gray-black cylinder of smoke rising.

''That's a new fire,'' Hazel said. ''I'm sure it's still

safe down in the canyon, but we better monitor this closely.''

Right then Jo couldn't have cared less about the fires. She was too busy accusing herself of gross stupidity.

She should have listened to that voice that warned her not to succumb to Nick's charm, good looks and flattering campaign to win her over. For in fact, those who had constantly measured her against her mother and found Jo lacking, were absolutely right. She saw that clearly now. As clear as bedbugs on a clean sheet, as Hazel often phrased it.

So clear it hurt all over again as if it had just now happened.

Her eyes filmed, and only with great effort did she hold back the tears.

Men might be sexually attracted to her, but obviously she had nothing to hold them after their lust was spent. Call it charisma, feminine mystique, whatever—she didn't have it nor a clue how to get it.

Well, all right, then. If she had been man-wary before, now she was washing her hands of them completely. A future spent in singles' bars and casual one-night stands was not her idea of romance.

No more being kissed in corners by married men, no more ''convenience sex'' for horny con men like Nick, either. Sure, she enjoyed the sex just as he did. But for whatever reasons, men didn't suffer the blows to their self-esteem that she did.

Suddenly Bonnie's voice, more impatient now, again jolted her back to reality.

"Hey, Jo! When are you gonna come to the party? This isn't a bathtub, you know!"

With a stab of guilt, she realized they had reached the frothing rapids and the raft was bouncing around like a cork, in part because she wasn't doing her job with the paddle.

"Sorry," she muttered, putting her back and shoulders into it.

Bonnie softened. "It's okay, but keep your head up from here. Day after tomorrow it won't be for practice. We'll all have to depend on each other, and no space cadets need apply."

Bonnie seldom lectured, and it only made Jo feel even more ashamed that her distraction had pushed her into it. She forced herself to pay attention for the next hour and a half.

"Good work," Hazel praised them as they hiked back upriver toward camp so the girls could change into dry clothing. "Only, remember that today there were no big rocks to contend with. Tomorrow, when you get about halfway down the Chute, you'll encounter a stretch of huge boulders. Just remember what Dottie told you before. If you fall into the river around rocks, don't fight the current. Go with the flow, and it'll most likely take you around the rocks."

Believe me, Jo thought in grim silence, I'll follow your advice. I already know how it feels when I crash into a rock.

The wind gusted against her wet skin, making her shiver.

But she wasn't worried about the dangers ahead for her in the rapids. Surviving the fear-inspiring Chute was kids' play compared to surviving her own wayward heart.

Fifteen

"**H**ere comes the cavalry, boys!" Nick called out to his team, pointing toward the sky. "Saved by the Canadians!"

Just south of the firebreak Nick's team had finally finished, a royal-blue transport helicopter hovered above the treeline. Orange-clad members of an elite smoke-jumper team from Alberta fast-roped down, sent in to relieve the Hotshots.

"So what?" complained Tom Albers. "HQ is sending us right back to Sector One without a day off."

Sector One, on their working maps, included Lookout Mountain and Crying Horse Canyon. Normally, after working day and night on special assignments like this rescue of Fort Liberty, a team got at least one day off.

Now, however, a potential new danger loomed. The weather station at Eagle Pass was predicting a potential "inversion" situation over the Bitterroot country—a unique set of atmospheric events that, in mountainous terrain, could act almost like a giant bellows on forest fires. In the worst-case scenario, even the smallest smoldering hot spots could be whipped into raging fires in a matter of hours.

"You think our fearless leader cares about time off?" Jason Baumgarter answered Tom, aiming a sly glance at Nick. "The man is in love, dude. He's champing at the bit to make more melodies with his hot little music teacher."

Assuming she's still here, Nick fretted, not even bothering to toss insults back to his second-in-command and his radioman. Based on what Jo had told him, the women should be here through tomorrow, when the younger women were supposed to raft the river.

They might have left early, perhaps discouraged by the fire news. Nick had no idea if evacuation plans had been issued yet to the general public. Or maybe something had changed with Jo. Of all the times to suffer a forced separation, it had to be right after they'd made love.

Even before the Canadian team members had hiked up to their positions, Nick instructed Jason to radio for their own transport.

In no time at all the Hotshots were once again setting up camp on the slope just beneath Bridger's Summit.

"We've still got six hours of good light left," Nick announced to his team. "The command center is worried about all that old growth at the north end of Crying Horse Canyon. Because of local topography, if we get an inversion situation, that part of the canyon will turn into a wind tunnel. We'll start thinning it out. Time is critical, so we'll fast-rope in. Be ready to stage out in—" Nick checked his watch "—in twenty minutes."

That would give him just enough time, if he hurried, to see if Jo was up at her cabin.

She wasn't.

In fact, both cabins were deserted. But at least the three cars were still parked in the lot, so they hadn't pulled up stakes and left yet.

Fighting back his disappointment, Nick took the stub of pencil from his pocket and dug an old cash-register receipt from his billfold, using the back of it to write a little note:

"Jo—stopped by to see you. Will try again later. Nick"

He glanced quickly around the clearing and decided to leave it on the redwood picnic table, weighing it down with a stone. He hated leaving such an impersonal note. "Love, Nick" was really how he wanted to sign it, but he found he longed to say the word more than write it.

Looking forward to seeing her later, Nick hurried back down the slope toward his camp. Already he could hear the chopper approaching from the command center on Copper Mountain—his ride to work.

"Slow down, Jo!" Hazel teased her friend. "Us old fogies can't keep up!"

"Us young ones, neither," Bonnie complained. "Why so gung-ho all of a sudden, Lofton? Are you training for the Olympics?"

The situation now, Jo realized as she stopped so the rest could catch up, was a direct reversal of their first day up here, when she was the one hurrying to keep up with Hazel.

But all this was deliberate. After wallowing in self-pity because of Nick's sneaky departure from the park, Jo had "bucked up" and transformed her attitude.

Okay, so her torrid tryst with Nick Kramer wasn't the smartest thing she'd done all year. She was determined to get over it and move on.

Now she was throwing herself into the outdoor activities with a vengeance, bound to forget Nick and justify Hazel's confidence in her.

Day nine, their last day before the floating final exam, as Hazel called the swoop-for-your-life, had been set aside for confidence-building and wilderness instruction. In the morning the girls ran through a special "circuit course" installed by the state university, a trail with numbered stations including climbing obstacles, balance logs, scramble nets and rope bridges, all safe but physically and mentally challenging.

It all kept Jo mercifully busy and focused on something besides Nick. But the brief break for lunch at midday gave her too much time to recall his face and touch, the feel of him inside her, the crushing rejection as he apparently slipped out of town like a thief in the night. Taking her heart with him, despite her safeguards and defenses against men like him.

"Jo," Hazel admonished, moving up beside her in the little clearing where they'd stopped to eat, some remote place well over on the western slope of the mountain, "drink some of your water and slow down a little. You're looking a little peaked today."

"I thought you brought us up here to toughen us up," she retorted aggressively. "Not to mother-hen us."

Hazel, in a rare show of surprise, backed off. That afternoon was devoted to a three-hour hike that took them off the mountain slopes and down into the canyon floor. Their destination was the site of an old Blackfoot Indian summer camp.

"This spot isn't mentioned in any of the tourist guides," Hazel explained, "because it was mainly just a work camp where they smoked and dried fish for the winters, not being a tribe that favored pemmican. We're gonna do it, too, on the same racks they used. It's fun."

Jo asked questions and pitched in with an enthusiasm she knew was excessive, yet for her necessary.

The others noticed it, too, and exchanged glances—or so it seemed to her. She hated this self-consciousness she now felt, which left her feeling literally beside herself, as if she was watching herself trying to cope.

And she definitely hated and resented their pity. Hated it most of all.

''Smoke's not bad at all on this side,'' Dottie said to Hazel late that afternoon when they were ready to hike back. ''But look how it's massed toward the river.''

''Yeah, I noticed,'' Hazel replied. ''I meant to follow the fire news closer today, but we've been on the move and I didn't get to it.''

She didn't bother to add that earlier when she heard all those choppers on the far slopes, it occurred to her Nick might still be in the area, after all.

However, Hazel wasn't about to mention it. Her instincts advised her to just let this one play itself out.

''We'll catch up on fire news tonight,'' Stella promised. ''Any signs of trouble, we cancel the swoop.''

''Oh, there's signs of trouble already,'' Hazel said thoughtfully, her gaze fixed on Kayla. ''Human trouble, that is.''

Dottie's grand-niece was rinsing her hands in the nearby stream, getting rid of the fish gunk, as she called it.

"You and me, Hazel," Dottie remarked, "have tied our thoughts to the same rail. Ain't Kayla being a model mountain gal these past couple days? At least, compared to the way she was?"

"Mm. Like maybe she's nursing a guilty conscience?"

"No fair, you two," Stella complained. "What do you know that I don't?"

"Nothing you can burn a brand into," Hazel admitted. "But something doesn't quite add up here. I'm thinking we better stand by for a blast, because something is due to blow."

The last of the day's sunlight was bleeding from the sky when the tired women finally returned to their cabins on Bridger's Summit.

Jo was sliding her backpack under her bed when Hazel came in and handed her a scrap of paper.

"Found this on the picnic table," the older woman informed her without any additional comment.

Her heart racing at the knowledge that he was still in the area, after all, she read the two-line scrawl.

It was a note from Nick. But in her present mindset, the note was not unlike a red rag to a bull.

Sure, he wanted to see her again. He was horny again, no doubt and she was the easiest game in town.

Much later, when none of this would matter, she would realize that it was her strange mood—exhausted, defensive, angry and hurt—which caused the ill-fated night. Despite her relief that Nick wasn't really gone, her disappointment in him was still too strong.

"Big deal," she said, crumpling the note into a little wad. "So he stopped by. What's he want for that—a gold star?"

"No," Hazel retorted pragmatically. "He wants to see you."

"'See' me? I'm sure he does. I'm just wondering, where was he two days ago?"

"Well, have you asked him that?"

"Why should I *have* to ask? I was ready, I waited. He's the one who blew it off."

"Honey, you don't know—"

"We'll need water for supper," Jo interrupted her friend. "I'll be right back."

I sure *do* know, Jo fumed as she went outside and grabbed the water jug. I know all about being some man's low priority.

After the physical and emotional closeness she'd shared, or thought she'd shared, with Nick, there simply could not be any excuse for not letting her know why he stood her up. That kind of carelessness, especially after her failed romance with Ned, was intolerable, period, end of discussion. Better solitude than a casual lover.

She was so absorbed in her thoughts that she hardly noticed the gathering dusk along the winding path. As she stepped out onto the stone footbridge, a familiar voice behind her made her draw up short.

"Jo! I just missed you topside. Hazel told me you came down here."

She spun around and watched Nick approach her, smiling uncertainly. In the grainy, dying light his face seemed pale and curiously incomplete—a blunt reminder she'd made love to a virtual stranger. This misery now was her reward.

She aimed a noncommittal stare at him. "Yes, here I am," she said casually.

Now that he was closer, out on the bridge with her, she saw how dirty and rumpled he looked, smelled the sweat of labor on him. It made her think a bit more about him, even though she'd had two days to stew in her own juices, and her resentment toward him cut deep.

"Hey, you okay?" she hazarded.

"Yeah. I know I look beat." He glanced ruefully at his smoky, torn attire.

Reaching for her, he bent to kiss her, but her instincts raged. She turned her head.

He let go. "What's this?" he asked, frowning, his eyes darkening with worry.

"Nothing."

He stared at her. "You want to ease off, don't you," he stated woodenly.

Inside, she released a moan of frustration. Now that she'd made up her mind to act sane again, he was going to entrap her. But there was no way she was going to tell him how much she wanted *not* to ease off. That conversation was his responsibility. Until she knew he wanted more from her than just sex she was going to keep her mouth closed along with her legs.

Hiding her hurt and anger, she moved toward the pump.

He stopped her with a hand on her shoulder.

"Hey," he said, sounding confused, "you got my note, right?"

"Thanks, I got it," she replied, shaking off his hand. In the waning sunlight, her angry eyes flashed like molten metal.

He stared at her, his expression cloaked. "Then what is it?"

She vowed not to show or feel anything until she was well up the hill and away from his view. "Look, it's just that I've had time to think, and this isn't what I want."

"What you want?" he echoed, his voice finally yielding to his exhaustion. "Well, out with it. What do you want?"

"I'm not trying to be unfair here. It's just that I— I want…" She turned around and faced the brook. Desperately trying to focus her mind on anything but the sting in her eyes, she finally stammered, "I—I want something, I mean, *someone,* a little more steady, I guess."

He moved up behind her and pressed her back against him. His arms crossed over her stomach like a steel cage.

Unbidden, need surged in her. If truth be known,

she wanted him, right then and right there, dirt, sweat and all, and the world be damned.

But it was clear now that he knew more than she did. He'd predicted they'd never be friends because sex would always be there between them. Unfortunately, sex wasn't enough when one wanted love and commitment.

"Look," he groaned, his cheek against her hair, "I know things have never been steady for me." He paused and his hold grew tighter. "All I've ever gotten out of this life was a fistful of air. It's become the thing I'm used to, but that doesn't mean I don't want more. I want you to know I'll take more if I can get it."

She couldn't believe his words. It was as if he was talking about candy, and if it was available, he would take as much as he could grab, whether it was chocolates, or peppermints, or both.

And it was the punishment she deserved for being so impetuous, for giving in to her loneliness. She'd had no business getting involved with any man, let alone this one, who touched her every weakness. Now that she was hurt, she had no one to blame but herself. Nick Kramer was who he was; she couldn't change him, couldn't make him want something he didn't. So it all must end, here and now. She couldn't give him another chance to lacerate her heart.

Bitterly she confessed, "Well, that's just it. You see, I don't want to be your port in the storm."

Shaking her head, she pulled away from his warm

embrace, still unwilling to let him see her face and the silent tears now streaming down her cheeks. "But don't worry, sailor," she choked, "there's always another port around." Her voice breaking, she began toward the cabins, ready to jog there if she must in order to get far away from him and the hurt.

He shouted to her, his anger and frustration growling through his words, "Napoléon was dead right. 'The only victory in love is to walk away.'"

Sixteen

Jo gave little thought to the river-rafting expedition awaiting them just past dawn on their last day in the Bitterroot National Forest. She knew, of course, that it was an important and final rite of passage for the Mountain Gals Rendezvous. But mostly she welcomed it for the opportunity to focus on something immediate and demanding.

Something besides Nick Kramer and her emotional torment. She didn't want to just push him out of her life, yet neither could she make herself open her arms to him and accept his leavings. Need warred with pride, and so far neither one seemed up or down. Just a miserable limbo of indecision.

The women set out for the river and missed hearing the radio news bulletin flashed throughout the region:

"We interrupt regularly scheduled programming for this emergency fire bulletin from the national weather station at Eagle Pass. Contrary to all expert predictions of a routine fire season in the Bitterroot Forest, ideal fire conditions have emerged in the past few hours. Known as an atmospheric inversion, the freak wind currents have already sparked several new and dangerous blazes in the north end of Crying Horse Canyon.

"All visitors to the Bitterroot National Park, as well as residents east of Hanover Creek, are now under immediate evacuation orders. Only essential park employees and firefighting personnel are authorized to remain in the designated area until further notice."

Shortly after the first broadcast of this warning, ranger Mike Silewski showed up to warn the women personally.

He found both cabins deserted.

Silewski shouted into the surrounding trees, but got no response. Frowning, he tacked an official evacuation notice to the door of each cabin. Then he thumbed on his handheld radio and "broke squelch," alerting Nick Kramer's radioman.

"Better put Nick on the horn, Jason," Mike said grimly. "I think we have a situation developing here."

"There they go, out of sight around Dogleg Bend," Dottie reported, watching the younger women's progress through field glasses. "They'll hit their first rough stretch soon."

"They'll be fine," Hazel insisted as the three older women headed back toward their summit camp. "I personally think this is the best bunch of gals we ever brought up here. True grit."

"Well, now," Stella said. "Will you look who's headed our way."

"Nick Kramer," Hazel said quietly, watching the grim-faced smoke jumper hurry toward them along the path. Three of his men were with him.

"I think I might give that young man a little piece of my mind," Hazel added.

But Nick gave her no time for that. In fact, he started speaking without even greeting them.

"Hazel, the park's being evacuated. We've got big-time wind inversion over the north canyon, fires breaking out all over down there. Have the girls taken off yet?"

At his words, an icy hand squeezed Hazel's heart. She exchanged a shocked look with her companions. The north end of the canyon was well out of sight, although Dottie had fretted earlier about the new smoke forming in that direction.

"Oh, no," Nick muttered quietly, reading the look on Hazel's face.

"They just went around the bend," Hazel replied. "No calling them back now."

"Hazel, I won't sugarcoat it," Nick said urgently. "That north end of the canyon is thick with old growth that burns like rocket fuel during a wind inversion. And even being in the water won't save them, because flames aren't the chief danger. In a box canyon like that, once the trees higher up start to burn, you get complete oxygen depletion at the bottom.''

So they'll asphyxiate, Hazel realized in horror. The girls were in a dirty corner, all right, and look who put them there. She thought of the old saying: Success has many fathers, but failure is an orphan. Well, this orphan was her baby, and she owned up to it. She'd had misgivings about the fire signs, yet ignored them. How many times had she told herself to heed that little voice at the back of her mind?

But blame wasn't the issue right now. Saving the girls was.

''So what's the plan?'' she demanded.

''It'll have to be Monument Rock,'' Nick answered. ''That's the last place accessible along the river before they hit the Chute. Once they pass Monument Rock, they *must* go on to the canyon floor. There's nothing but sheer rock walls on both sides.''

Hazel nodded. ''Monument Rock it is. We were just now heading up to get our cars and drive there on the fire trail.''

''Good. We'll go with you. Once we get there, though, you ladies will have to hang back beyond the treeline while we work our way down to the river.''

''They'll be moving fast by then,'' Tom Albers pointed out. ''If smoke's thick down there, they may never see us.''

''We'll run a rope snare,'' Nick decided as both groups, women and smoke jumpers, began hurrying up the path to the summit. "We can't let them slip past us. The way that timber was going up just before our team was pulled out of the north canyon, no living thing will have a chance on that canyon floor."

The four rafters had easily weathered two stretches of white-water rapids within their first hour on the river. Now, feeling more confident, Bonnie bent close so Jo could hear her above the roar of the water.

"Piece of cake so far," the hairdresser said. "But look how thick and dark those smoke clouds ahead of us are getting."

"Yeah, I didn't notice those when we took off," Jo replied. "It's hard to tell from here just where they're coming from."

"We'll know better in a few minutes," Kayla shouted from the thwart behind them. "When we get through the bend coming up, we'll be able to see well into the canyon."

To her surprise, Jo had quickly learned that Hazel was right; so far, anyway, the "swoop" downriver had indeed been fun. The four women had proved a competent team with their paddles, and the exhilaration of hurtling along, plunging and weaving and bobbing, at times made them laugh like little kids in bumper cars.

Even so, Nick stayed on the fringe of her mind, a presence too important to be forgotten. But at least now, as her confidence built rapidly, she could rationalize the beginnings of acceptance.

A thistle cannot produce figs, she reminded herself, and a narcissist can truly love no one but himself.

"Get ready back there!" Bonnie called as they edged closer to the end of the long S-bend they'd entered. "I hear more rapids up ahead!"

"Oh, my God!" Kayla exclaimed as their raft shot through the last of the turn, giving them a panoramic view of the canyon below them.

And the fire that raged through it like Armageddon.

Jo glanced ahead and felt her heart plummet and her blood seem to carbonate with fear.

"What are we going to do?" Kayla cried.

"We can't keep going!" Bonnie yelled, close to the verge of outright panic. "It's like a blast furnace down there!"

"Quick, Jo," Sheryl asked urgently. "What do we do?"

Jo had read the phrase "rendered witless by terror." Now she knew exactly what it meant.

Below them, spot fires raged on both sides of the river, and farther down, past the Chute, a huge inferno covering dozens of acres roared out of control.

"We can't keep going!" Bonnie repeated. "Look, the fire is even jumping the river! We'll be literally floating in flames!"

"We can't head to shore here," Jo said, somehow finding her voice. "Look how steep the banks are— we'll never get tied off. But the current is getting stronger as we descend toward the Chute, so we'll have to make our try soon—the first place we see where we can nose in and get to the shore.''

Even as she spoke, dark, acrid smoke wafted to her nostrils, bitter and sharp, carrying with it the hint of a terrible death.

Seventeen

―――

"Okay, Hazel," Nick said tersely from the back seat of her Fleetwood. "This is as far as you ladies go. Do *not* drive beyond the treeline. This whole area could go up like a fireworks store."

Nick and Tom piled out of Hazel's car, Jason and Brian out of Dottie's station wagon right behind.

"Look!" Jason shouted, pointing out over the river. A news helicopter was circling the area. "The vultures must have been monitoring the radio and heard about this."

Ahead of them, still out of sight, the otherwise steep banks of the Stony Rapids River leveled out briefly on the east side, site of the tall sandstone pinnacle called Monument Rock. About fifty yards downriver from there, however, began the steep final descent of the Chute—"final" in every sense of the word right now, for the entire north canyon was a roaring wall of wind-whipped flames.

The searing heat and oxygen depletion could kill a human being within minutes.

The only hope for anyone on the river was to detour here and escape to the high ground while there was still oxygen.

Nick only hoped they'd reach them on time.

At first, after they entered the trees, Nick and the other smoke jumpers made good progress as they made their way toward the river, easily avoiding the hot spots. But suddenly Jason called a warning. "Nick! The fire's closing in behind us! Pincers drift!"

Despite the adrenaline spiking his blood, Nick felt his heart turn over in dread.

All smoke jumpers had one rule drummed into them from their first day of training: *Never surrender your escape route.* "Pincers drift" was code meaning that the only way to safety was being pinched off. Under the usual rules, at this point smoke jumpers gave up and retreated while they could, fire be damned.

But rules didn't matter now to Nick. Jo and three others were about to die a terrible death if they weren't stopped at Monument Rock. He knew he could never live with himself if he let the woman he most wanted to spend his life with perish.

He coughed as burning smoke filled his lungs, then

exchanged a quick glance with the others. He knew they were thinking about the same thing he was: the deadly Mann Gulch and South Canyon fires, charred graveyards littered with the ashes of smoke jumpers who'd surrendered their escape route.

"You guys get the hell out!" he shouted. "You ain't paid to go on suicide missions!"

"What, and let you get all the glory? We're dogging your heels, sweetheart!" Tom hollered. "Let's get it done!"

Time was not on their side.

As they neared the river, more and more hot spots forced them to keep seeking safe routes. Nick began to fear the girls would shoot past before he and his crew even got to them.

"Screw it!" he finally shouted when yet another detour sent them in circles. "Go to foil, gents, and follow me!"

Without hesitation, all four smoke jumpers broke out their foil ponchos and threw them on. Then, with a silent prayer to Saint Jude, patron saint of lost causes, Nick led his men at a full charge into the teeth of the fire.

"I'm jumping out!" Kayla cried. "It's our only chance."

"No!" Jo snapped without hesitation. "That current will take you all the way down to the canyon floor."

"We've got life vests, and—"

"Jo's right," Bonnie argued. "Look, Kayla, look at those banks! Even if you could fight your way to the side, you'd never be able to climb out. You're better off in the raft."

"At least it's a plan!" Kayla said, nearly hysterical now. "All we're doing now is waiting to die."

"We have a plan," Jo insisted above the gathering roar of the approaching Chute. "But it's going to take every one of us acting as a team, Kayla, do you understand that?

"We're only gonna have one shot at getting off the river at Monument Rock," Jo went on. "We do it just like we practiced, sharp turns up above. On my command, we all stick our paddles straight down, close to the raft on the right side. With luck, that will throw us toward the east bank."

"You with us, Kayla?" Sheryl demanded.

"Kayla, are you *with* us?" Jo repeated, on the verge of slapping the panicking Texan.

Something in her voice must have gotten through.

"Yes," Kayla promised. "On your command."

Jo had begun to notice some alarming bodily symptoms as the river carried them lower: increasing headaches, dizziness, difficulty breathing, requiring deeper and deeper inhalations to satisfy the lungs.

"Oh, God," Bonnie said beside her, so low only Jo could hear. "We're running out of oxygen."

"Just a few more minutes, Bonnie," Jo encouraged her. "Stay focused, we'll be making our move. We're only getting one quick shot at it, so be ready."

* * *

Nick's desperate gambit paid off. All four smoke jumpers made it to the river with no serious burns. He had no idea yet, however, if they were on time to intercept the raft.

"There's nothing to tie the rope to on the other side," he told his companions. "So two of us are going to hold it. Tom, you take this bank. I'll swim across and brace myself in that clutch of rocks. We've got to keep it about one foot above the water, so it grabs the raft but doesn't knock the girls into the river."

He coughed again, blinking smoke from his eyes as he turned to the other two. "Brian and Jason, you guys wade out as far as you can. If we can slow the raft, you two can help wrestle it in. Main thing is, make sure that if any of them fall into the river, you grab them."

Nick pointed downstream, where a plume of mist marked the beginning of the Chute. "Unless we can pull a rabbit out of the hat, guys, they're screwed, glued and tattooed. So are we if that current takes us."

Nick was already wading out into the swift-running river as he issued these words. Just before the current began to bowl him off his feet, however, he saw the raft suddenly shoot around the bend ahead, its four whey-faced passengers poised to plunge their paddles.

Good, they were planning to try an escape here.

But damn it, they were approaching too quickly! He'd never get the rope across.

"Forget it, Tom!" he shouted above the roar of the river. "Here they come!"

Nick realized now that his plan was no good, anyway, for the current was too strong. It took all his strength to keep from being washed down.

There could be only one plan now: wait for the women to do their thing, then try to block the raft if they failed.

But in fact, Jo's plan worked too well. Nick heard her shout, "Now!" and watched all four of them move as one, plunging their paddles. However, the motion did not just send the raft right toward the flat bank—it threw it into a spin.

At least they were closer to shore. But Nick saw they were in danger of being sucked right back out into the middle of the river.

"Jump!" he screamed, fighting hard now just to stay afloat.

All of them leaped into the churning water, and Nick saw Tom and the others racing out to help them.

Jo, however, had been the last one into the water, and she was farther out by the time she jumped.

A flailing tumble of arms and legs, she hurtled past Nick.

In a desperate effort, he lunged, grabbed hold of one of her ankles and began the struggle of his life to break the death grip of the raging current.

Then, inch by torturous inch, Nick fought his way

toward the bank, Jo in tow. By the time they collapsed in the shallow water, safe, he was so exhausted that every breath ended in a little groan.

Kayla, her nerves stretched tight, began to sob almost hysterically when she realized they had survived the river. But tired as they all were, the most dangerous part still lay ahead. Wordlessly, the four smoke jumpers put their foil ponchos around the women.

Nick took Jo's hand. "Hazel's waiting just past the trees. One quick run and we're safe. Ready?"

She squeezed his hand. The lump of fear in her throat made it difficult to talk just then, but she nodded.

"Ready," she managed.

In her eyes, Nick was all hero during the difficult climb out of the canyon. His instructions to the other men were swift and absolute, and through years of trust and experience, the men followed him as if he were their god.

Bonnie and Jason got caught in a sudden flare-up. Nick raced down the incline and fought for their escape route. Then and there, Jo realized she'd fallen in love with him. Steadiness or not, when he'd disappeared behind the curtain of flames, he was all she wanted.

And when he reappeared with the two through the smoke, it was all Jo could do not to run to him and leap into his arms like a schoolgirl.

At the top of the ridge all media hell had broken loose. Ambulances were arriving in case they were needed, and two helicopters battled to see who could get the best shot of the rescue.

But the eight who had fought their way to safety barely noticed. They were too exhausted.

Hazel shooed the cameras away and made sure for herself no one was injured. Then she hustled Jo and Nick away from the media circus to the back seat of her car.

The matriarch drove her Caddy like a skilled barrel racer, dodging ambulances and satellite trucks in her haste to put them behind her.

Jo was grateful for the peace. Staring at Nick, she knew she had something to say that was long overdue.

"Forgive me," she whispered to him.

His eyes looked impossibly beautiful in a faceful of soot. "Forgive you for what? You didn't know about the inversion."

She shook her head. "No, forgive me for being so selfish. I do want someone steady in my life and if you're the one, I really think we could be happy." Her heart tightened. "But if you don't want that, if you can't make that work for you, then I want you to know I understand. You're a hero, Nick. What you do out here is important. If you need five women to take the edge off, I can understand that now." She gave him a sad little smile. "I just wish I didn't care for you so much so I could be one of them."

He reached out his hand.

She pressed his palm against her cheek. The calluses felt good. Just another indication of how capable and strong he was.

"I've never needed five women, Jo. Just one." His voice grew husky. "Just you."

She stared at him, hardly daring to hope. "I'm not good at sexual games, Nick. It needs to mean something—"

He didn't let her finish. Pulling her to him, he kissed her deeply, stroking her face with his scraped knuckles. "I've always dreamed of one woman to love, and one woman to love me, forever. You're the first woman I've ever met, Jo, who let me see forever."

With that, he wiped away the tears from her cheeks. Then he kissed her and kissed her, never seeing the smug satisfaction on Hazel's lined face in the rearview mirror.

Eighteen

"So this is the famous Mystery Valley," Nick said in a deeply impressed tone, enjoying a stellar view of it from the twelfth-story balcony of the area's finest resort hotel. "No wonder you and Hazel love it. Crops, grassland, forest, and all of it surrounded by mountains. I've seen a lot of the American West, but nothing to top this."

Jo pointed toward a huge pasture dominating the distant view.

"You can't actually see the town itself from here except for the spire of the Methodist Church. But that's one of Hazel winter pastures. The Lazy M occupies one-third of the valley. Right now her cattle are up in the summer pastures in the foothills."

"She's the big nob in this town, and to think," he said with that wolfish grin she'd grown to love, "*we're* driving around in her Caddy and using her plastic. I feel like a VIP."

"You complaining?" Jo teased. "Or maybe you're just tired of the company?"

"Yuck, sick of it," Nick said, literally lifting her off her feet as he pulled her into a deep, breath-quickening kiss.

Nick and his three companions had received the customary one week off, at full pay, always granted to smoke jumpers who received the coveted Lifesaving Award, as the four of them had. But a grateful Hazel, who had wept with gratitude when all eight of them emerged from the trees safely, had insisted that wasn't enough.

"Both of you kids are heroes to me," she effused to Nick and Jo, "and you're gonna have a heroes' holiday, on me."

Nick could have named anyplace in the world, so Hazel and Jo both took it as a promising sign when he immediately voted for "this Mystery Valley that seems to produce such remarkable women."

It hadn't been quite the private getaway they'd envisioned, however. Their faces were still too fresh from the recent, dramatic rescue photos and subsequent media interviews—hotel staffers and other guests recognized them, and there was always an awkward "celebrity stir" each time they appeared in the dining room.

It was all so silly.

They wanted none of it. A cabin in the woods and a well for water was all they needed.

Jo finally broke from the long kiss to say, "You know, Hazel really likes you. She sure has been banging the drum on your behalf."

"No accounting for taste, I guess. The only question is, how do you feel about me, Ms. Lofton?"

"Well, you're pretty good in the sack."

She said this deadpan, and they both laughed.

"Seriously," she said, "I agree with Hazel's first impression of you."

"Which was?"

"That you're a keeper."

"If Kayla hadn't absconded with my note, you might never have thought otherwise."

His arms tightened around her, and she shivered, thinking how fragile their beginning was, how full of fear and flight. It was a wonder any two people could get to know each other.

She looked at Nick and realized how easy love was once found. But before that, it was a lot easier to talk herself out of trying to love than to give it a shot. "All Kayla did," she said, "was give me an excuse not to risk my heart. I didn't want to be used like Ned had used me."

She framed his handsome face with her palms. "But after our escape, as brave as I was in the river, when I saw you I realized I had to be brave one more time. I couldn't push you out of my life completely. I would have lost so much.''

He grinned. ''Kayla gave herself the hiccups, she was sobbing so hard when she confessed. You mad at her?'' he asked, pulling her close again.

''Oh, I tried to be, but she was so miserable I couldn't stay mad. What we went through on the river...it sort of bonded us, I guess. You know, we actually hugged and made up before she and Dottie went home.''

Jo harbored no bitterness, for the trip into the wild had ended with two key discoveries, both very welcome: that Nick had not deserted her, after all, and that she possessed all the confidence and inner strength she'd ever need. Or in Hazel's earthy terms, she had a backbone to go with her wishbone.

Neither one of them had spent much time fully dressed the past few days. Her hand moved down inside the folds of his robe.

''Um, I see *this* fireman is feeling sparky.''

''Hey, don't start something you don't plan on finishing.''

''Who said I don't plan on finishing?''

She knew him well enough by now to know he had at least two types of smile: one, quick and easy, that he used as a defense against others getting too personal; another, charming and roguish, that could instantly turn her on as it was now.

''I want you,'' she whispered urgently, giving his arousal an inviting squeeze.

He never did require an engraved invitation—he easily scooped her up into his arms and carried her back to the queen-size bed. He untied her silk robe and shucked it, along with his own.

Moaning with the building intensity of their sudden passion, still unslaked after several days, they sank onto the bed, Jo rolling over to straddle him.

He grabbed both breasts, but she toyed with him, sometimes letting his mouth take her nipples, sometime making him do without as she rocked herself against him.

Finally, when his arms went around her hips and stilled her, she knew there was only one way to go.

She bent his hard length to the perfect angle and lowered herself onto him, feeling him deliciously filling her. Crying nearly incoherent words of pleasure and encouragement, she began moving her hips, letting his hands take full measure of her breasts as she rubbed along his length.

His head turned from side to side as the pleasure built. Faster and faster, harder and harder, she rode him, her own ecstacy building as he cupped her breasts, kissing each nipple in turn, nibbling them just a little and making them swollen and hard with pulsing blood.

Their lovemaking had shown several moods, and right now their shared mood was pure possession. She had no desire, this time, to prolong her pleasure, to draw it out teasingly. Instead, she, like him needed a thorough coupling and intense explosion of release.

They had driven each other to the edge of control. The moment of possession came like a massive wave, the climaxes wracking her body into surrender. She cried out just as he, in a few deep, final lunges, released himself inside her, his pleasure as hard and greedy as her own.

Much later, when they had each drifted back to the surface of awareness, he murmured in her ear, "You know, Hazel has already assured me there's a good job waiting for me here in Mystery."

Jo, almost forgetting to take her next breath, replied, "Think you might take her up on the offer?"

"If I was ever tempted, it's now. She's pretty convincing when she says there's no better place on earth to put down roots and raise a family. I'd like to give it a try."

She sat up in bed and looked at him. She remembered how he'd pulled her to him after they'd made it safely to Hazel's car. Their faces black with soot and exhaustion, he had made her feel as if she was the most beautiful woman he'd ever seen. There was nobody besides her, he'd told her, and so far he'd done nothing but prove it again and again in the weeks since.

She'd sworn when they parted that fateful day, he'd said the three magic words—"I love you"—but the frenzy afterward made her think it must have been her imagination.

"Nick Kramer, are you thinking of settling down?"

He gave a wary sideways glance. "Only here. Only with you. Otherwise, I'm lost. All I'll have is that fistful of air."

"So you're asking me to marry you and help raise that family of yours?" Her face was taut with wonder.

He caressed her breast and pulled her back down into the bed. "I sure am. So what's the answer?" He gave her that slow, sexy smile she had come to know was hers alone.

She kissed his lips. "The answer is yes, but just a warning, though, Hotshot—life around here isn't as exciting as smoke jumping."

"I beg to differ," he countered, lowering his mouth to hers. "There's plenty of fire in you."

Almost three months after the rescue on the Stony Rapids River, a brand-new blanket of powdery snow covered the Bitterroot National Forest like an ermine cloak. It was the first real accumulation of the winter.

Ranger Mike Silewski slowly prowled the park's main access road, the Blazer's front snowplow lowered for action. While he worked, he kept the radio tuned to the midday news report out of Helena. The newscaster closed with a human-interest story that instantly riveted Mike's attention:

"Wedding bells will soon be chiming for a Mystery, Montana, music teacher and the heroic smoke jumper who saved her life. And Hazel McCallum's world-famous Lazy M ranch in Mystery Valley will soon host its fourth big wedding in recent memory.

"In a ceremony slated for late May, Joanna Lofton, twenty-five, and highly decorated firefighter Nick Kramer, thirty, a Colorado native, will tie the knot on a relationship that began a few months ago when they were briefly thrust into the national spotlight.

"Last August Montana residents joined millions of other Americans in a tense, minute-by-minute vigil after Kramer and three comrades risked almost certain death to rescue Lofton and her fellow rafters from fire-ravaged Crying Horse Canyon.

"Neither one of the engaged couple was available for comment regarding their plans. But cattle magnate Hazel McCallum, seventy-five, granted a brief interview from her home. She confirmed that Kramer, now a special consultant to the Montana Bureau of Forest and Land Management, has become a resident of Mystery Valley. He is also teaching forest conservation at Summerfield Community College near Mystery.

"'I'm on the board of regents for the college,' McCallum told reporters, 'and happily the other regents share my belief that our instructors should be working professionals who've done more than just read some textbooks. Nick's course has been wildly popular. We're lucky to have him. In fact, he's just the kind of man this valley needs.'

"Ms. McCallum hinted, at the end of her interview, that she expected a substantial number of weddings in Mystery's near future.

"When asked to elaborate, she declined, saying

only: 'Oh, I'm a sentimental old romantic, is all. It's just a hunch.'''

* * * * *

Don't miss the next book in
Meagan McKinney's
MATCHED IN MONTANA *series!*
Look for THE COWBOY CLAIMS HIS LADY,
coming in March 2003 from Silhouette Desire.

Available in March from *USA TODAY* bestselling author

LINDSAY McKENNA

A brand-new book in her bestselling series

MORGAN'S MERCENARIES

DESTINY'S WOMEN

An HONORABLE WOMAN

From the moment Commanding Officer Cam Anderson met Officer
Gus Morales, she knew she was in trouble. The men under Gus's
command weren't used to taking orders from a woman, and Cam wasn't
used to the paralyzing attraction she felt for Gus. The ruggedly
handsome soldier made her feel things a commander shouldn't feel.
Made her long for things no honorable woman should want....

**"When it comes to action and romance,
nobody does it better than Ms. McKenna."**
—*Romantic Times*

Available at your favorite retail outlet.

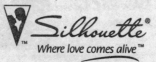

Silhouette®

Where love comes alive™

Visit Silhouette at www.eHarlequin.com

PSLMHW

Silhouette® Desire®

presents

DYNASTIES: THE BARONES

An extraordinary new miniseries featuring
the powerful and wealthy Barones of Boston,
an elite clan caught in a web of danger,
deceit and…desire! Follow the Barones
as they overcome a family curse,
romantic scandal and corporate sabotage!

Don't miss one of these 12 compelling
love stories by your favorite authors.

Enjoy all 12 exciting titles in DYNASTIES: THE BARONES:

Available at your favorite retail outlet.

Silhouette®

Where love comes alive™